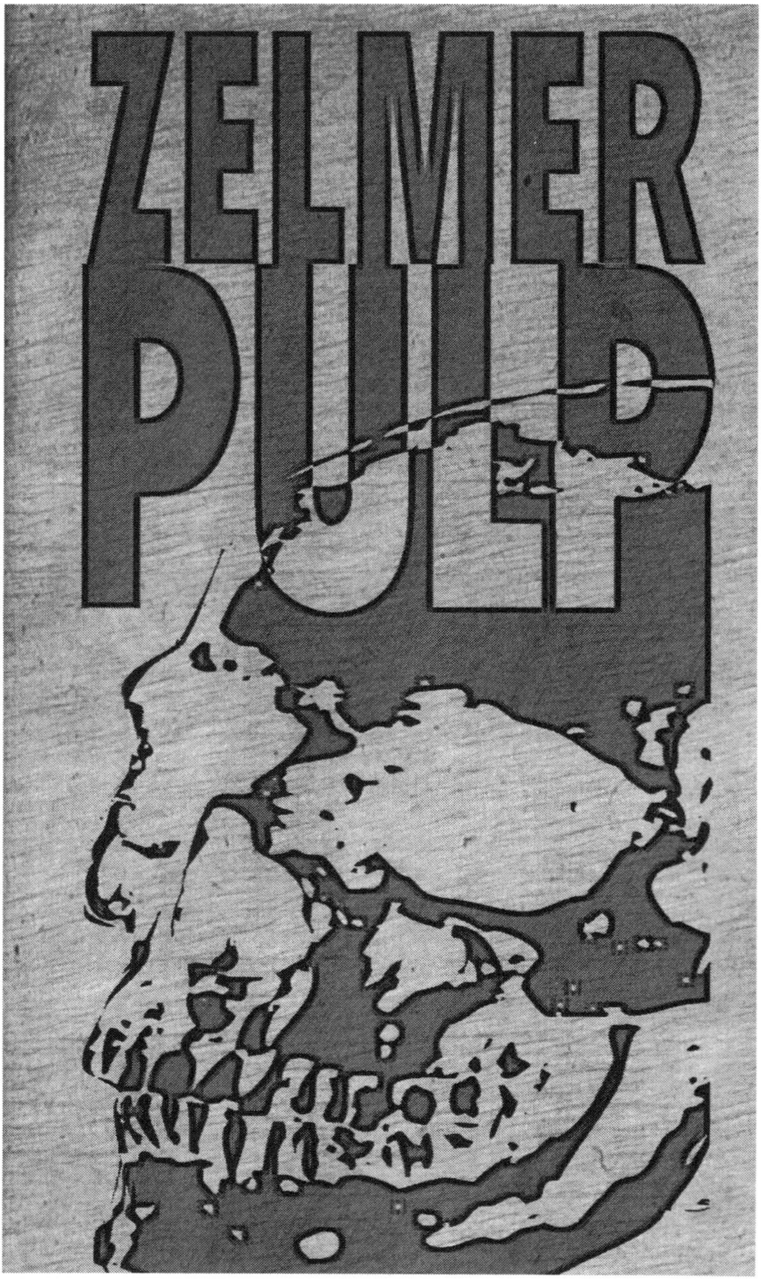
ZELMER
PULP

Maybe I Should Just Shoot You in the Face

Volume One

Contents

Paul   **D.**   **Brazill**

Shots in the Dark

Paul D. Brazill

Crime fiction is easily and readily sliced up into subgenres, especially these days. We have the cozy, the murder/mystery, the detective story, the police procedural, the hardboiled. Or the social realism of Brit Grit, which wears its dark heart on its blood-stained sleeve like a call to arms to the dispossessed, disenfranchised and desperate.

And it's also categorized by country too—Scandinavian crime, for example, is expected to have a very different flavor to the Italian or French variety.

Noir, though, to quote Spinetingler Magazine's Brian Lindenmuth is, "More like a style of fiction." More elusive, perhaps. Like a murder glimpsed from the steamy window of a passing train.

The origins of 'noir' as a definition of a sharp sliver of crime fiction goes back to the mid-1940s when the French publisher Marcel Duhamel cleverly packaged American pulp fiction—from the likes of Raymond Chandler, James M Cain, Jim Thompson, Cornell Woolrich—in black covers, as the imprint Série noire. And since then it has also been tied like a noose to the cinematic versions of those books. Films that painted the world with light and pitch black shadows.

Ostensibly crime fiction—or skirting its razor edge—noir is a taste that's as black and bitter as an espresso or a shot of moonshine-whisky. Noir, for me, is all about mood. And a dark mood at that because, as Otto Penzler once said, "Noir is about losers." For writers and fans of noir, we are all in the gutter but some of us are looking at the abyss between the stars.

Last Exit

Chris Leek

People say life begins at forty. It doesn't. The fact is it's been going on all the while, only you've been too busy to notice; forty is just the age when you start to worry about how much of it you have left. I looked up at the Williamsburgh Tower just as the hands on the clock there crawled past midnight and Monday turned to into Tuesday. Like death and taxes, time is relentless.

In a few hours the world would wake up to a brand new day. Maybe for some it would hold the promise of something better, for me it would be just mean more dive bars and dead ends. Kelly had been my shot at a happily ever after and now she was gone; choked out in a Brooklyn alley like a Hitchcock Heroine. I shoved my hands in my pockets and kept walking. An empty beer can rattled along on the breeze beside me, keeping me company with its hollow chatter for a few yards before jumping off into the gutter. I didn't really notice it until after it was gone. That's always been my problem.

I paused to light a cigarette in the shadow of a five-story walk-up. The mellow bluesy sound of a detuned guitar tumbled down the fire escape from a loft somewhere above. I leaned up against the grimy brownstone and listened while I smoked. It was the soundtrack to a lazy summer on the shore, not winter in the city. I shivered and drew deeply on the smoke, sucking the glowing cherry a little closer, hungry for its heat. I thought about heading back to the hotel and trying to sleep, but every time I closed my eyes I saw the dark smudges ringing Kelly's throat; the empty impression of a killer's hands staining her skin with one final, lasting insult.

"Hey mister, you spare some change?"

I looked around and saw an old rummy by the service entrance, clinging to a dumpster like it was a life raft. I pitched my cigarette and walked across.

"Have you seen her around, friend?" I asked, showing him Kelly's picture—the one where she's on the boardwalk looking out at the ocean, her hair billowing out behind her like a bolt of red silk. He peered at it running a grubby hand through the wild tangle of his beard.

"Yeah, I've seen her. She works the corners up on 9th," he said like he was making an apology.

You can't choose who you fall in love with any more than you can make them love you back.

"Thanks buddy," I said and peeled him of a couple of singles and then thinking better of it I added a ten spot. "Be sure to get yourself a hot meal along with the bottle."

He nodded his thanks and shuffled into the night. I watched him go, thinking there was one more hard luck story that nobody wanted to hear. I turned up my collar and started towards 9th Street. A direction wasn't a destination, but it was a start.

*　　*　　*

I didn't know what line of work Kelly was in when I met her, and in spite of my job, I wouldn't have cared. She was everything I could have wanted, but we barely lasted six months together, not much—not nearly enough. The last time we were together was at Easy Earl's out near the Parkway. We were only a couple of drinks into the weekend and already burning in the same old firefight. She said something. I said something back. She stormed out. I got drunk. We rode that broken merry-go-round a lot, each of us not dealing with the problem in our own way. Kelly liked to run from it and I preferred to hide in a bottle. You could say we were just too different for it to work, opposite ends of the scale and all that. But deep down, where neither of us really wanted to look, we were exactly alike.

By the time I made it home she had gone, for good this time. She left a note pinned to the refrigerator, it just said: *If you ever really loved me, then you'll understand.* I loved her all right. I guess I should have told her that more often. I never understood though. I still don't. It's a goddamn mystery to me how I managed to fuck things up so badly. Perhaps in the end I didn't, not completely. When they found her in that alley, she had my number written on the back of her hand, like maybe she was planning on calling. Guys like me only get what they deserve and that doesn't include second chances, but that hasn't stopped me tearing myself to shreds with *what ifs* ever since.

*   *   *

Rain had started to lash the streets by the time I reached 9th. It seemed like it had rained a lot since Kelly left me. I dodged behind a checker cab and crossed the street to shelter in the doorway of a 24-hour Laundromat. There was only one customer inside. She was eighteen-going-on-a-hundred and meth-skinny. Her thrift store coat had a tear in the sleeve and a style that hankered after the days when disco was king. I pushed open the door and went inside.

"Excuse me, miss. Have you seen this girl?"

She looked up at me with empty eyes, charred and shattered like the windows of a burnt out building. She glanced at the picture in my hand, shook her head and went back to watching clothes spin around the dryer. I had this crazy idea that I should put my arm around her and tell her how it would all work out someday. But both of us would know that was just a crock of shit. When you reach a certain point, life starts working like gravity and from then on, you only go down—we both knew that too. I thanked her and went back out into the storm. The yellowing sign on the door said: *We Never Close.* In this town that worked just as well for old wounds as it did for fresh laundry.

*   *   *

At first, the local cops liked me for Kelly's murder. Sure, why not, I would have too. I was twice her age with a string of bad relationships in my wake and a couple of assault charges on my record that had never gone to trial. I was exactly the kind of loser who might fall for a twenty-something hooker and then whack her when she decided she didn't want to fuck old men for free anymore. One phone call to my Major in Atlantic City cleared all that up. He confirmed I was Jersey PD and more importantly that I was standing right next to him at the time their radio car called Kelly in as DRT— *dead right there.* She was still warm and I was over a hundred miles away. That left the local boys all out of ideas. They had nothing. Neither did Kelly; no family to miss her and no one to claim her body. Without Kelly I had nothing either, apart from for a picture that broke my damn heart every time I looked at it.

*   *   *

I huddled in the doorway. Rain drummed on the pavement and thunder rolled down Park Slope like a gutter ball. Beneath the storm, spiked heels beat their own rhythm on the wet sidewalk.

"Are you looking for company?"

She was stunning in a hard kind of way, her finely cut features all made up of Asian angles and edges.

"What's a nice Irish girl like you doing out on a night like this?" I asked.

It was an old line and she must have heard a thousand lame variations of it a million times before, although it still got me a smile that was somewhere between uptown girl and back street lover; a smile like that must have meant something to someone, once.

"Rain doesn't matter, not if you've got bills to pay." she said and twirled her umbrella.

"What's your name, Irish?"

"What do you want it to be?"

I held out Kelly's picture. She took it and the rain washed the smile from her face, leaving only a well-worn sadness and a hint of rouge.

"What are you some sort of cop?" she said thrusting the photo back at me.

"Yeah, but I'm not a cop around here. This is personal."

She looked at me hard, an arched eyebrow posing the question.

"Kelly and me, we were—" I stopped myself, there didn't seem to be any words for what Kelly and me were... friends, lovers, soul mates? We were all of those and none of them. I know that sounds dumb, but that's just how it was, although now it was something else.

"Shit, you're him. You're Kelly's cop, the one she met in Atlanta," she said.

One time, back when I was still in uniform, I stopped a bullet during a stash house raid. I was on point, first up the stairs. I took a .38 high in the chest and woke up in Memorial Hospital two days later. Her words hit me in much the same way. They told me there could have still been a chance for Kelly and me and that was a hell of a '*what if*' to add to my list.

"Actually it was Atlantic City," I said pushing the hurt away and sticking only to the facts—Joe fucking Friday would have been proud.

She shrugged as if everything south of the Jersey Turnpike was a foreign country. "Kelly told me *all* about you, officer." she said coyly, cocking her head over to one side giving me a glimpse of cheekbone you could shave with and perhaps also of the girl she might have been before the streets claimed her. "I kind of thought you'd be, you know, younger."

"Time catches you up," I said, "unless somebody else catches you first."

She looked around and then took a step towards me, her umbrella shielding us from anyone who might have cared to watch. "You should go talk to that bastard Manny. He was leaning on Kelly for a cut of her action."

"And?"

"And she told him to go fuck himself."

That sounded a lot like Kelly, she never took any shit from me; I doubt she took it from some low-life pimp either. "Are you saying this Manny character is the one I'm looking for?"

She glanced anxiously up and down the street. "Well, it ain't like Kelly choked on a pretzel, honey."

"Where do I find him?"

"*Romero's* over on Carroll, but if he finds out it was me who told you, then…" She left her sentence unfinished and for a moment it hung pointlessly between us, like Christmas lights in August.

"He won't, I promise," I said reinforcing the statement with my eyes.

She held my look for a moment, taking stock and passing judgment. "Maybe you are the kind of guy who keeps a promise, but I wouldn't know, I never met one."

I tried to give her money, but she folded my hand closed, which made me feel like a piece of garbage, and then held it in her own, which made me feel better. Not much, but like the old drunk by the dumpster, it gave me something to cling to.

"Kelly was a friend and those are hard to come by," she said.

I nodded. Cops and whores; we had that in common.

She smiled the sort of smile that could melt hearts like ice cream on a hot day, stood on tiptoe and brushed her lips against mine. "Make things right," she whispered.

The echo of her footsteps faded into the night, leaving me with the lingering promise of her perfume and a cold empty feeling in my guts.

*   *   *

Romero's was a low rent pick-up joint in a low end neighborhood. It was all buzzing neon out front and cocktails with suggestive names inside; the kind of place where the sad and the lonely came to drown their troubles like kittens in a sack, before pairing off to fuck each other's brains out. It was a home for the kind of misery that loved company.

Things were winding down by the time I got there. Only two or three couples conspired in the row of shadowy booths. I took a stool at the bar; joining a scattering of late night drunks, all of them hoping the answers would magically appear at the bottom of their glasses if they stared at them long enough.

The bartender came over, laid down a napkin and looked at me expectantly.

"Jameson, straight," I said.

"Don't have Jameson, Bushmills alright?"

It wasn't, but the alternatives all came with chunks of fruit floating in them, and that isn't drinking, it's just getting wet.

"Manny around?" I asked as the bartender set down my drink.

He nodded towards the door. I turned to see a young kid walking in with slutty looking arm candy on either side of him; one blonde and the other dark like he was having trouble making up his mind.

That was the kind of problem a lot of men wouldn't mind having. Down here you could rent your own dilemma for $500 an hour.

The trio breezed past me took seats at the far end of the bar. Manny ordered the drinks and then started feeling up the brunette. His hands walking all over her tight little body while he talked shit with the blonde just to hear the sound of his own voice.

I was expecting a hard-bitten flesh peddler, not some damn college drop out. No doubt the kid thought he was a player, but to me he was just another parasitic pimp; a guinea worm in a designer suit. I never heard of any girl telling a high school guidance counselor she wanted to fuck for money. Making a living on a filthy mattress in some by-the-hour motel room isn't anybody's idea of a dream job. The pimps were the only ones who got rich off that kind of work. I downed my drink and grimaced; it wasn't only the protestant whisky that left a bad taste in my mouth.

Manny laughed and leaned in close to the blonde, nibbling on her ear as he whispered something. She giggled like it was the cutest thing ever, but I caught the look in her eyes and it told a different story. It was all an act. She was only doing what she had to. I ordered another drink and pretended not to notice the generic brand name peeking out from under a carelessly placed Bushmills label on the bottle. In a place like Romero's, everyone did their share of pretending.

The brunette got a call on her cell about three drinks later, not long after both the girls got up and left. The wait had given me too much time to think and not enough to get drunk. Manny settled his tab. I did the same and followed him out. The Browning Hi-Power I'd ripped from a Jersey banger the previous week felt heavy under my jacket, like I needed to empty out some of those homemade hollow points and lighten the load. It would have been easy to grease the bastard there and then, but Manny wasn't something I intended to rush. I had all night.

The storm had blown itself out and a cold damp mist was seeping in the streets off the Hudson. It was the kind of weather that suited both my plans and my mood. Manny turned left and slouched off down the street toward a late model Cadillac. That figured. Just once I'd like to meet a pimp who drove a Prius. I moved up behind him as he fumbled in his pocket for keys and pressed the business end of the nine into his ribs.

"Let's you and me take a ride, kid."

"What the—"

I brought the gun up and cuffed him on the back of the head. "No, you don't talk, you just drive."

*   *   *

I directed him west, toward the docks. Corner stores and apartment blocks gave way to smashed concrete and steel shutters daubed with illiterate graffiti that nobody over the age of sixteen could read. When we hit the river I made him take a right, along the broken, pitted asphalt of a dead-end street lined with boarded up warehouses on one side and row upon row of rusty containers on the other, all patiently waiting for ships that had sunk along with the economy.

"Look man, I got ten large stashed in the trunk. It's yours, just take it," he said.

"I don't want your, money."

"What then, got to be something, blow, girls…boys? I ain't gonna judge, I mean it takes all sorts right?"

I looked across at Manny, his hands nervously pawing the wheel. In his world everybody got bought and sold, it was just a matter of price.

"All I'm looking for is truth and enlightenment."

"What truth? What are you one of those religious freaks?"

"Yeah, I'm the goddamn second coming. Now, stop the car."

He pulled up just past the last container, next to the legs of a giant crane; the rest of it lost somewhere above the glow of the streetlights. I reached over and took the keys from the ignition.

"Get out, let's take a walk."

The mist had upgraded itself to fog. It cut off the noise of the city, leaving only the gentle sound of water lapping the dockside. I marched Manny down past the containers and out on to a wooden pier cluttered with discarded rollers of cable.

"That's far enough," I said stopping him halfway along.

He shoved his hands in his pockets and stood hunched over against the cold. Ten feet below us, the black and moody Hudson oozed reluctantly towards the ocean. On the far side, the Manhattan skyline was no more than a rumor.

"We're on 53rd Street."

"So what?"

"Nothing, I'm just saying we're on 53rd Street, a couple of blocks over from Bay Ridge Flats."

Manny shifted his feet uneasily, his eyes darted left and right, looking everywhere but at me.

"Hand it over, you sneaky little runt."

"Hand what over, man?"

I worked the slide on my Browning, chambering a round. "Give me your phone, asshole."

He pulled the cell out of his pocket. The screen was lit, showing me the line was open. Twenty years a police and I let him pocket dial the cavalry like some wet-nosed rookie. I snatched the phone out of his hand and stamped it under my foot. I had to assume the clock was running now. I took out Kelly's picture and pushed it towards him. He looked at the photo and quickly turned away.

"You know her?"

He shrugged. His expression remained flat and unreadable— street survival 101.

"Did you kill her?"

He just stood there, shivering with the cold and maybe something else.

"Answer me dammit!"

He flinched like I'd just made to hit him. "L-look I got connections, man. Maybe you should walk away now, while you—"

I jammed the pistol into his cheek, forcing his head back. "Maybe I should just shoot you in the face, how would that be?" He started to mumble something. "Huh? Speak the fuck up."

"I said just fucking do it then," he sobbed.

His whole body was shaking. I tightened my grip on the gun. All I had to do was squeeze. Just another pound or so of pressure on the trigger would be enough to smear Manny all over the pier. Some people got to leave their mark on the world; he would only leave a stain.

"Tell me the truth," I yelled in his face.

"I...I..."

A dark patch spread out around his crotch and urine drummed on his expansive Italian shoes. Irish had told me to make things right and this didn't feel right anymore. It felt like murder. I lowered my gun.

I looked from the trembling Manny with his piss-soaked pants to the banger's nine in my hand. The serial numbers had been filed off and the bullets scored so as they would deform on impact. It was a weapon designed for only one purpose. In Manny's world it was all about price and this was one I couldn't pay. I tossed it in the river.

Manny sniffed up a snot rocket and stared at me wide eyed. His mind desperately trying to work out what kind of trick I was playing on him.

I wanted the truth and now I had it; killing him wouldn't change a damn thing. Kelly would still be dead, the world would still be fucked up and I would still have to go on living in it, alone. I pulled

Manny's car keys out of my coat, dropped them at his feet and walked away, my hollow footsteps echoing along the wooden pier.

"Y-you fuck," he called after me his voice cracked and broken. I ignored him and carried on up the slope toward the containers. "I'll...I'll kill you for this, man." Talk might be cheap, but he still couldn't pay the freight. "Just like I killed that whore."

I stopped cold and spun around. Manny had followed me down the pier and stood on the dockside. He was shaking more than ever; an emotional junkie hopped up on fear and anger.

"Yeah, that's right." He screamed. "That bitch squealed like a pig when I choked her out."

My hand shot inside my coat and found only the empty holster. Manny saw me go for a piece and he turned to run. His foot caught in a spool of cable, his legs tangled around it and he tumbled headfirst into the Hudson.

I ran down to the edge of the dock just in time to see him break the river's oily surface. He was spluttering like motor trying to throw a rod and grabbing at the water as if it were something solid that he could take hold of. The kid was no swimmer. For a second his eyes locked on mine as he struggled—just long enough for them to burn into my skull—and then he was gone.

I don't believe in fate or karma. In fact, I don't believe in much of anything. I just know that time catches up with everyone sooner or later. I buttoned up my coat and started walking, keeping myself one step ahead of it.

Dawn limped painfully into the eastern sky; agonizing over the birth of another thin winter day that would only last to mid-afternoon and make you wonder why it bothered showing up at all. I was tired, hell I was exhausted, but I didn't go back to the hotel. I knew that Kelly would be waiting for me when I closed my eyes and I had a feeling that maybe now Manny would be too. I needed a reason not to sleep, any reason would do. A pretty one would do best.

I went looking for Irish and finally found her, stirring coffee in a window booth of a mom and pop diner, a couple of blocks over from the Laundromat. Daylight suited her; it made her look softer, sort of smoothed out her edges. She didn't seem all that surprised to see me.

"You look like shit," she said.

"Funny, I was just thinking you looked pretty good."

"Did you make it right?" she asked as I slid into the seat opposite her.

"No, not really, I don't think it will ever be right, not for me anyway." I said fishing a pack of smokes out of my pocket. "But nothing will come back on you, Irish."

"At least now I know what a man who keeps his promise looks like," she said and sipped her coffee.

"Yeah, he looks like shit."

I waved over the waitress and ordered a coffee. I offered to get her another, but she declined and we sat there for a while without speaking. Words didn't seem to matter right then. I lit up a cigarette and peered out at the street. The condensation on the diner's window made the city looked softer too.

"So what happens now?" she asked finally, pulling my gaze back inside.

"I've been wondering that myself. I think I'll take Kelly back to Jersey with me. My old man bought me a plot next to his, up at New Lawns Cemetery. I figure she can make use of that."

"Won't your dad mind?"

"Nope, he'll be glad of the company. He always was a sucker for a pretty face."

"Oh I'm sorry, I thought..." she shifted uncomfortably in her seat.

"Don't be. He's a long time gone." I said, trimming my ash.

"Ain't we all," she said and took a cigarette from my pack, her cherry-colored lips doing more to promote the habit than any billboard I'd ever seen. I snapped open my lighter, spun the wheel and leaned across the table to set her on fire.

"What about you?" I asked.

"Well, officer," she said pausing to send a cloud of bluish smoke up towards the fluorescents, "you could take me home with you too. It will run you two hundred, but I can guarantee it'll be worth it."

I didn't doubt that for a minute. "Here," I said and handed her my photo of Kelly. "I'd like for you to have that."

She took it; that same old sadness showing up on her face again. "Thanks," she said and turned the picture over in her hand. I had written my phone number on the back. "What's this for?"

I crushed out my cigarette and got up to leave. "That's just in case you ever need another friend, Irish," I said and started towards the door.

"Wait, I don't even know your name," she called after me.

The smile felt strange on my face, almost as if it belonged to someone else. I guess it had been a while since I'd used it. I turned and shot it her way. "What do you want it to be?"

Omega Man

Benoît Lelièvre

Some things are just too great to last.

You can climb Mount Everest, but you can't build your house there. You do what everyone does if you're driven and lucky enough to achieve something so great. You sit on top of the world, let the moment of unspeakable beauty sink in and when your soul is filled with the splendors of this Earth, you go back down. Because you can't live where it's too perfect for oxygen, where every gust of wind is powerful enough to send you down the jagged landscape, down to your inevitable death.

Something was off about Briana. It had been a tremendous couple of months, we didn't know each other very well yet, but we were having fun together. I thought it was what mattered. But you can't keep to yourself what every man wants. Not if you're just a regular guy like me. I thought I understood and accepted that reality, but I lived every day like a celebration of our awesomeness, like it was a perfect object, frozen in time. I decided to ignore the growing twinkle of mischievousness in her eyes. The increasing delay of response to my texts. The sudden multiplication of "girls night's out." That shit doesn't lie. No sir, it never does. Not even if you decide to ignore it.

"David, we need to talk."

God, she was beautiful that day. She had her hair cut short and dyed blonde about a week before. Her tanned, smooth skin glowed, soaked in the daylight coming from the patio door of my parents' kitchen. She wore just a tank top and yoga pants, but she rocked it like other women rock bikinis on June 1st after spending 6 months doing expert level Zumba classes. She had been out until the wee hours of the morning and fell asleep at my side with her clothes on. Leather jacket. High heels. Smeared makeup. The whole nine yards. That shit doesn't lie either.

The latent dread in her voice betrayed her intentions. I was a pedestrian trapped on the freeway in rush hour traffic and I had about half a second to choose my fate and save myself a painful end.

"All right, cut the crap," I said, pouring myself a glass of orange juice to keep my debonair composure. My hand was slightly shaking and I hoped she didn't notice. "Who is it?"

That fucking twinkle again. She lowered her gaze. A bad girl smirk blossomed on the corner of her mouth. My heart pounded the drum parts of Slayer's *Raining Blood* through my chest. I could hear it in my ears.

"Stuart Price," she said, biting her lip.

Of course. Stu. Fucking. Price. I must've rolled my eyes or something because it set her off. "Don't be so fucking condescending, David. Let's be adults about this and end things smoothly, okay?"

"Whatever," I said, struggling not to add *whore* at the end of my sentence.

"What? You don't think I owed you the truth? I shouldn't let this drag on and make both of us miserable?"

"Don't talk to me like I'm the bad guy, here. If you want to do the right thing by me, pack up your shit and leave. Don't come back here. Don't call me. Don't text me. Just don't."

Briana didn't let me finish my rant. She scoffed in disbelief and stormed out, picking her clothes off the floor, offended like I pulled up her dress in public. It was a good guy rant. I had an ending in mind and banked on her being smart and sensitive enough to find it beautiful. My witty, intellectual side won Briana over and I thought a desperate plea could keep her by my side. Show her I could offer her what Stu Price never would. But I'm always expecting too much out of people, constantly breaking my own heart.

Stu Price was one of these people who seemed to hover over the challenges of common mortals: a freak athlete who could do double back flips off the diving board when he was twelve years old, a golden gloves champion boxer with a hard, chiseled body today. He sported a ten-pack of abs on his worst day, without even working out. I saw him box a couple times, everyone in town did. He was one of these peculiar, once-in a generation talent. He mastered his craft so well, seeing him in action gave you that life-affirming feeling that you ought to do something great with your life. That being a bystander to greatness was beneath you, however little human potential you may possess.

Shit, Stu wasn't even such an asshole. I went to high school with the guy and knew him to be fairly decent, if a little alpha sometimes. They were perfect together. It pissed me off, but it was the truth. Their bodies looked like they were made for one another. Barbie and Ken. I didn't know if they had anything more profound than genetic Darwinism going for them, but it still made more sense than what we had.

I wanted to mend fences with Briana before she'd hop on the happily-ever-after express to Priceville, but she left by the front door, without saying goodbye. I could've sworn she was crying.

*   *   *

That cunt.

That motherfucking cunt.

There aren't a lot of good things about getting dumped, but you DO get a lot of extra time for yourself. It's a strange feeling of freedom, like someone pushed the reset button with your life and you don't know what to do with yourself anymore. After Briana left me, I spent a lot of time pacing around in my bedroom, listening to late-era Black Sabbath records and dropping for pushups whenever I had unexplainable spike of nervous energy and rage.

There had to be something more to this. Something I didn't understand. Why was she crying when she left? Why did she run away like this instead listening to what I had to say? I played the morning of our breakup in my mind over and over again, looking for clues and hidden meanings. Briana was the fucking world champion of hidden meanings: her words concealed her desires and her every movements were meant to show me the path to her secret garden. She only gave herself to men who could crack her code.

 Maybe it was the isolation or the malnutrition talking, but it all pointed to the obvious and painful evidence—I've been played. The code was changed on me and I got locked out.

Bitch could not do that to me.

I wanted her back. I wanted her to cry and beg. Ask for my forgiveness on bended knee. I wanted her to love me until it hurt.

I went for a walk, one night. I didn't have a destination set in mind. I wanted to shed the restlessness that kept me awake all the time, so I walked passed my old neighborhood and went downtown. Over there, I kept walking until my legs ached and the inside of my jeans was soaked with sweat. I ended up in a desolate industrial area that I didn't even know. There was an oil refinery nearby. Large, grey buildings that seemed like garages to me. There were a couple of shops, too: electronics, landscaping, tires, that sort of stuff. I was hungry and thirsty and there weren't any cheap dives in sight.

It's right there, at the heart of my own, personal oblivion, that it dawned on me. I walked into a shoddy, second hand electronic boutique and bought myself a cell phone with two sim cards. An iPhone 4S, exactly like the one I already have.

"You have to call phone company. Deregister. Register to you," the guy behind the counter said, in a heavy Pakistani accent.

I gave the guy my best boy scout wink and walked out of his boutique with a grin on my face. The excitement of my idea carried me home, like a pair of angel wings. At home, I plugged the phone into my laptop and found the number through iTunes. It belonged to a poor bastard named Erik Angelson. When I Googled his name, I found a man living upstate. I had bought exactly what I was looking for: a stolen phone.

Briana was a romantic and a princess, so for her I became the Omega Man: a tragic, nameless and evanescent lover, and the last boyfriend on Earth. The last and only man she would need. The first text message I sent her went something like this:

Don't let these men put out the flame that burns within. You're worth more than them, Miss Briana. You're worth more than the treasures of this Earth...

She didn't respond to that one. I didn't expect her to. It was the only message she ignored, though. In this world, it's difficult for anybody to stay insensitive to someone who sees you the exact same way you've always wanted to be seen – who tells you what you always wanted to hear about yourself.

I had a strategy to win Briana back. I wouldn't try to compete with Stu. Not physically, anyway. He was bigger, stronger, more handsome and capable to thoroughly kick my ass. I was going to become immaterial. An idea. Something that experience could not and would not ever fulfill. You can't build your house on top of Mount Everest, but if you're crazy enough, you can climb it more than once. It's not because you've reached the pinnacle of human achievement that you can't aim even higher. Who stopped Michael Jordan after winning his first championship? My goal was not to win Briana back anymore; it was to make her obsessed with me.

Romantic black ops like a motherfucker. What else was I supposed to do?

*   *   *

The following months were slow, impossible, passionate and unreal. I didn't know if they were good or bad, but at least they were interesting. My texting strategy developed into a full blown online romance that existed within the confines of Briana's computer. Our torrid and passionate discussions, all of our empty promises were punctuated by photographic evidence of her growing involvement in her relationship with Stu, on her Facebook timeline.

Briana dropped out of school in her junior year at Rutgers and became assistant manager at the local funeral home. Mr. Jordan, the lone undertaker in town, had buried his only son Felix the previous summer and it seemed like Briana had taken the lead in the gold rush to his succession. Stu turned professional and signed a television deal with ESPN to appear on *Friday Night Fights* after winning his first two bouts by TKO. Together, they moved in a modest bungalow that belonged to Stu's parents. Briana Fraser was moving forward with her life and documented everything online for the world to see. She kept the Omega Man in the closet of her adult life, like the nasty little secret that it was.

I spent entire nights at work texting and chatting with her. It's a game where there's a fine line between reality and the things you wish for. It's a strange netherworld of duplicity and romantic ideals. Briana lived her life with Stu during the day, and woke up at night to live the life the Omega Man mirrored to her. One night she wrote.

I wish you would take me away, O. Stop all this nonsense and take me with you, where time has stopped.

I'm always here, Miss Briana. Around the corner, looking over you from where you can't see me.

Sometimes I close my eyes and I can almost feel you. I can free the warmth of your presence and the electricity of your fingers caressing my cheek. You always go for the right side, so you must a lefty... but then I open my eyes and I'm all alone again, with a stranger sleeping upstairs.

You're not alone. Your reality is what you make it. If you can touch, if you can feel, it means that I'm with you always.

I want more than feel you. I want to look into your eyes; I want you to feel me too.

When the time is right, Miss Briana. When your inner light will shine the brightest, it'll be clear enough to see me.

I feel so lost.

I still have that conversation in my phone today and when I get depressed, I read it over and think what would've been if I revealed myself that night. I was on my way to her house when we had this discussion. Since I invented the Omega Man and sneaked back into Briana's life, I took on myself to put a dozen roses on her porch at least once a week, just to show her I was there, waiting. Everybody saw them: Briana, Stu, their entire neighborhood. My strategy was to put pressure on the relationship, let it collapse on its own and run away with the spoils.

I always moved at night, when the streets were empty and the normal people were sleeping. I felt like the world belonged to us then.

Briana became obsessed with trying to catch me in the act. She read near her living room window every night and peeked outside every two minutes. I arrived at her house a little past midnight. She was standing like an angel in the fiery glow of a floor lamp, completely naked. Her body was slightly different from what I remembered. Her hips and her thighs were fuller and she had lost the striking muscle definition that drove me mad with desire. Her small, perky breasts had become heavier and sagged outward slightly. She let her hair grow over the last eight months and cut it straight over the shoulders, with square bangs on her forehead. She looked different, more womanly somehow. She also looked like the weight of adulthood and responsibilities was driving her into the ground. Her beauty was still stunning, but she shined a different, more tragic light.

What I saw that night still haunts me today. She shoved her hand between her legs and started throttling herself. It was not a gentle or sensual gesture. She went back and forth and thrust her hips, like she was following the beat of a violent techno-industrial song. It was not pornographic either. She seized and writhed and grabbed handfuls of her hair, possessed by an invisible energy. I was horrified, but I couldn't look away. Briana was letting go, delivering herself to the Omega Man, or whatever she wanted him to be, in her fantasies. I don't know how long it lasted. Not more than a couple minutes, I'm sure, but it felt like hours.

She looked drained afterward. Physically and emotionally empty. She closed the living room lights and took shelter into the darkness of her house and that was that. I remained in the woods for a long moment, not knowing if I should bust through her door or run away. My heart was drilling holes through my eardrums and my legs felt rubbery. I had to lean against a tree to collect myself. I was confused; I had no idea what she was trying to tell me. I still don't.

I decided to leave the flowers on her porch anyway.

*   *   *

That night, I saw through the looking glass and into the heart of Briana's vulnerability. I had the nagging feeling that not only I wasn't supposed to see this, but it wasn't supposed to happen altogether. My strategy to win Briana back was based on appealing to her overbearing romantic side, but what I had witnessed wasn't romance or even sexuality. It was like watching someone fall into a bottomless pit after chasing an illusion for too long.

A couple days later, the portrait became a lot clearer. Briana announced that she was engaged to Stu. She posted another one of these hideous photo albums on Facebook, displaying photographs of the ridiculous rock Stu offered her, of themselves cuddling in the backyard, corny reenactment of Stu's Great Demand at the dinner table. I browsed through the album once. Then one more time. Then I started browsing Briana's photos frantically until I finally cracked her code: this was an ultimatum.

I used to call her baby doll when we were together. It wasn't something cute and spontaneous I came up with, it was a sex thing. Briana let go in the bedroom like no other girls I've been with. She didn't surrender control, she ordered me to take it. She liked it when I grabbed her throat, pulled her hair and fucked her in the ass. It made her squeal like a porn star when I did that to her. I'm sure no other man indulged her needs with the dedication and the abandon that I put into it. Not even Stu.

Once or twice, she lied flat on her stomach, asked me to fuck her from behind and played dead until I was finished. That's when I started calling her "baby doll." Because even I wasn't that fucked up. Briana was so good at this; I needed to constantly remind myself that I wasn't fucking a corpse. The nickname just stayed.

I had been a fool. Briana and Stu's relationship was never going to break on its own. She would call for help in her own coded language, but Briana would only surrender her body to a conqueror. I called her baby doll for so long, but I didn't actually "get" it. I was going to take her out of that house. I was going to put Stu Price out of competition permanently. I had to kill him or abandon Briana to her domestic purgatory.

I followed him out of his house at the first opportunity.

He walked outside of his house a little after sunset and stood in his driveway alone, gazing into nothingness. He wore a Gold's Gym t-shirt and beat-up grey shorts. First opportunity. I could walk around the yard and come from behind: BAM. Two in the dome. He would've never known what hit him. I could dispose of his body however I saw fit. I didn't do it, because I didn't want Briana to hear it. Even worse, see it. She was looking for a great wizard, a magician who could take her away from everything. Not a murderer.

So I waited.

Stu eventually snapped out of it and stepped into his car. I followed him through the deserted streets of the city. Another opportunity. I could've stopped at a streetlight and popped him right there, through the side door. My weapon was powerful enough to do that. But I knew intersections were a risk. Anybody could have been watching from the shadows and identify me. Besides that, I was curious to know where he was going.

So I waited.

He stopped at Wanda's, a local dive that became a Go Go Dancing Bar on weekends. It was a strange place where the waitresses became dancers like men turned into werewolves during the full moon. Tonight was not one of those nights. On weekdays, Wanda's was just another pathetic joint with sticky floors and dirty bathrooms. A lot was going on in that place, when the tourists and the thrill seekers were looking the other way. It was owned by some small-time lowlife mobster named Robert Mordecai, who used it to hold court and launder money.

Stu ordered at the bar and walked over to a booth on the far right of the room with no direct line of sight and beside the fire exit. Perfect.

So I invited myself. He didn't look surprised to see me.

"I order for you too. Lager, is that good?"

I sat in front of him and gazed into his eyes without saying anything. I wanted Stu to understand it was game over. He lost. I won. It was the end of the road for him.

"You know, I always knew it was you. All that time. Briana said it was impossible. She said you were way too self-involved and narcissistic for that. That you couldn't think beyond your own asshole, but you and I aren't so different, bud. We know how to get what we want. I think she just didn't want to put a face on her mysterious lover. That he was perfect the way he was," said Stu. I remained silent, but the muscles of my face must've shifted. "She's in the trunk of my car, Dave. I just needed to make a pit stop for courage. And to figure out what I'm gonna do with her, of course."

My heart into my chest and I had tunnel vision for a moment. His reptilian gaze was brimming with pride.

He threw the keys on the table, between us. The waitress, a cute, peroxide blonde in her late thirties chose that moment to drop our beverages. I slipped her twenty and invited her to keep the change.

"Take a look if you want," he said.

He was bluffing. He had to be. He wanted to drag me outside and shoot me, just like I intended to do to him. Stu and I had chosen the same night to end the Omega Man saga. High noon at the local dive.

"The difference between you and me is that I understood what Briana wanted. You kept trying to figure out what it was, but I knew that whatever guys like you and me could offer her would never be enough."

"Don't talk about her in past tense," I said.

I was scrambling for something to say—a course of action to take, but every flip and tumble I could make in my mind would inevitably come back to the here and the now—to the words that Stuart Price was saying at this table.

"She's gone, buddy and it's for the best. Briana was like a movie character. The greatest tragedy for her is that the credits never rolled after she got 'the guy'. It's over now, anyway," he said.

I pulled my weapon. Right there in the bar. Once again, he didn't look surprised. Nobody did. Stranger things happened at Wanda's. I reached across the table and grabbed Stu by the collar of his stupid t-shirt. I pressed the cannon against his left cheek, right under the eye.

"Don't you want to know why I proposed before I did it?"

Still, I couldn't talk. I had a million questions, but they all died in my throat. I could see nothing but bravado in his eyes. No indication that he was lying.

"I wanted you to know that you lost, Dave. That she died mine.''

I cocked the hammer and Stu chuckled.

"You're not gonna do that here. I know you're not. Not in front of witnesses and shit. You're not gonna throw everything away; it's not in your nature. Let's go see her one last— ''

"Wanna know something?'' I said. "I'll live. I'm going to wake up tomorrow and do everything I can to make sure the only thing people will remember about you is that you murdered your wife.''

I shot him in the face and ended his miserable life. The back of Stu Price's head exploded into sludge and dripped down the white leather of the booth. He died with a somber look, knowing he set fire to his crops for nothing and that gave me solace.

I radioed it in right away: "Shots fired. I repeat, shots fired. Suspect is down. Start an ambulance to Wanda's...''

I sat down and waited for the cavalry to arrive. I didn't have the strength to pick up Stu's keys and check out his trunk. I didn't have the strength to pick up my phone and call Briana either, to see if he was bluffing. I didn't matter anymore, anyway. I sat and drank my beer, thinking it was what oblivion felt like. Think it was what it felt like to come down Mount Everest with an unspeakable truth.

Give a Good Day

Isaac Kirkman

It was on one of these roads that Otto Antwerp's daughter Olivia was shot, or one day, years from now will be shot. Sorrow is circular that way. Otto stands in the afternoon light, groggy and clutching a fresh dog track race program. His nose is bulbous and sun-cracked. His white eyebrows perch over his dark eyes like a pair of albino crows clutching black apples. He lifts his straw hat, and wipes his forehead with a geometric-patterned handkerchief. The heat is clean of clouds or humidity, the Sonoran landscape flat and endless as a laser beam. The Yaqui congregating at the AJ Hayes Market wave at Otto as he passes.

Some days Otto makes his way to the blood bank downtown or to the University where the gunshots become yoga mats and praying abuelitas become MFA atheists. Daily moving on currents of memory, circular through the city to places he forgets are no longer there or are yet to be created. But today Otto moves through his old neighborhood, a space Google lists as dangerous—an outsider's description of another person's pain. All down the roadsides, crucifixes and bullet holes clump together with sun-eaten saints and discolored plastic flowers marking someone's sudden passage from this realm.

As Otto ventures toward the bus stop he eyes a young couple digging through the trash. When he had met them a year ago he had thought they were his wife and himself in youth— ghosts passing safely through the world, their movements hidden in mirrors and clocks. Now newlywed to the needle, the couple grows more haggard each time he sees them, looking past him as if they don't know him or he isn't there. He feels at times there are versions of himself in other worlds crying, using up all the tears he was allotted in this life before he got the chance.

He takes a seat on the enclosed bus stop bench a block from the community college. This time of year the school gives students a red balloon for each college credit completed. Otto could see students floating a few inches above the sidewalk, balloon or two in hand, and sometimes, graduates soaring up from the parking lot holding a fistful. Student by student ascending into the blue Ein-Sof. Race program in hand, Otto smiles as the sky fills with students holding red balloons, each vanishing from the ghetto upwards into the clouds.

He checks his pocket watch. Soon his daughter Olivia will step off the bus. Sometimes Olivia is twenty-four years old when she greets him, holding her son Oliver's hand as the bus wheezes away. Other times she is older than Otto. Last week Olivia was eleven, holding a red balloon when Otto picked her up at the stop. Love is circular that way.

The bus comes and goes and no one gets off. As night loosens daylight's tourniquet, junkies bleed from the city's wounds. Meth-pipes spark in economically abscessed buildings, blistered lips circling the mouth Hubert Selby's scream was searching for. Rows of addicts amble down the street, circling past Otto like grainy film projections. Their faces deflated, eyes like crumbling black roses.

Otto sighs, folds the race program into his pocket, red ink around the name of a dog called Give a Good Day, and follows the setting sun where greyhounds circle forever.

Once Upon a Time in the Woods

Brian Panowich

For Talia, Ivy, and Olivia

"Ouch! That fucking thing bit me!"

Micah chewed his lip to keep from laughing in his partners face.
The squirrel came out of the woods and attacked Aleksey as soon as
they started to take the package out of the backseat. It was the
strangest thing. Squirrels don't act like that, but as bizarre as it was,
it still stuck Micah pretty goddamn funny.

"Suck it up you big pussy, it's just a tree rat, how bad could it be? Hurry up and get in the house." Aleksey got a solid grip on his end of the package, and with a groan, he helped Micah carry it inside the cabin.

The two men gently laid the package down on the sofa, and Aleksey sat down in a huff to examine the wound on his foot. The damn thing did a number to his Achilles tendon. Blood was already starting to fill his sock. It would take forever to heal.

"Did you see that?" Aleksey said, not looking up from his wound.

"Yeah, yeah, I saw it, but focus. Call The Krolowa and tell her we have the package. Tell her we're at the cabin waiting for further instructions."

"What if it has rabies?"

"Then your goddamn foot is gonna fall off, and still nobody is gonna give a shit, now make the call." Aleksey didn't like being spoken to like that. If his foot didn't feel like it had been set on fire he would slap this young prick across the room. Instead he pulled out the burner phone and dialed the number.

After a short pause he spoke "We got the girl." Another short pause. "Yes Ma'am." Aleksey slapped the phone closed and tossed it on the oak coffee table.

"What did she say?"

"She say to wait."

"How long?" Aleksey didn't answer. He got up and limped his way across the cedar cabin into the bathroom to fish out the first aid kit.

Micah kneeled down in front of the linen-wrapped package on the sofa. "Can you breathe in there?" He heard a grunt that sounded a lot like "Go fuck yourself" spoken through a bandana gag.

Yeah, he thought, *she could breathe.*

*   *   *

Three hours past and Micah started to get restless. Aleksey popped a few Vicodin for his bite wound, and was snoring loud and wet in a big leather easy chair next to the sofa. The girl—tied up, gagged and rolled in bed linen—was surprisingly stoic. She shuffled a little every now and then, but not once did she try to get the men's attention. No pleading for release. No requests to go to the bathroom. Nothing. Micah had taken a number of these snatch and grab jobs from the Krolowa during his time in the states. They were mostly children of wealthy Americans, who would pay the ransom without ever involving the police. Once the money found its way into The Krolowa's pockets, the child would be released on the side of the road somewhere and everyone counted their cuts. Every gig was the same. Every child was the same. All spoiled brats crying for their Daddies and pissing their pants, but not this one. Even at the initial snatch up she didn't show any fear, just irritation. Aleksey took out the girl's Limo driver with a black jack to the cranium, stripped him, put on his clothes, and picked the girl up from school in her own family's car. When Aleksey didn't answer her questions and she realized something was wrong, she just steeled up. Even as the big sweaty Polish man gagged her and bound her hands and feet, she just glared at him as if the heat from her stare would be enough to free her. Aleksey was so freaked out by the girl that not only did he blindfold her, but he also wrapped her up completely in bed linen so he wouldn't have to look at her. Then he drove her to meet Micah who waited with the switch car. When Micah first saw the kid wrapped up, he was afraid to ask, but now he was beginning to get it. This little girl was fucking creepy.

The phone on the oak table started to vibrate and bounce lightly on the wood. Micah snatched it up and flipped it open.

"Yes…but I thought…Okay, one hour." He closed the phone and tossed it onto Aleksey's bloated gut and kicked his leather chair. The big Pole awoke with a start.

"Get up, we got the call."

"What did she say?" Aleksey yawned and rubbed his eyes.

"She said get the fuck up, fat man. We gotta move. We gotta be at the warehouse in one hour."

"But I thought…"

"Don't think; just help me grab this brat."

"I'm getting a bit sick and tired of the way you talk to me, Micah. I'm third in line to The Krolowa herself. I deserve respect from you fucking half breeds." Aleksey stopped talking when he realized that Micah wasn't listening. He was staring out the cabin's window into the open expanse of Jersey Pine. Something caught his attention and drained all the color from his face.

"What is it Micah?"

"Come take a look at this. You're not gonna believe it." Aleksey walked over to the window and opened the dry rotted yellow drapes so he could see out. Lining the driveway on both sides and blocking the car were hundreds, maybe thousands, of small animals. Not just squirrels, but possums, foxes, raccoons, chipmunks, and even a few groundhogs. They weren't scurrying around either like you would see animals do at an abandoned campsite. They were just standing there, staring back at the two men in the window—waiting for something. There were all kinds of birds visible in the trees too. Blue birds, Cardinals, blackbirds—a shit load of black birds—all perched and focused on the cabin.

"You have got to be kidding me." Micah said.

"I told you something was wrong with that squirrel. It has the sickness, the whole forest has the rabies." Micah just stared at the bigger man in amazement of how stupid he must be. Something was happening that he couldn't explain, but he knew for sure that rabies didn't affect everything from groundhogs to bluebirds. He didn't pretend to understand what was going on, but a pack of furry creatures was not about to sway him from his cut of the cash. His orders were to move the package, and if he wanted to get paid than that's what him and this big moron were going to do.

"Get the girl," he said, "I'll clear us a path." With that Micah grabbed a pump action Mossberg from beside the fireplace, and loaded it from the box of shells on the mantle. He racked the gun and stood to the side of the front door. Aleksey chewed a few more Vicodin and bitched about his throbbing foot before throwing the girl over his broad shoulder like a roll of carpet. Micah took note of that. The big fucker was tough. Maybe he should curb his tongue.

Micah took a step out onto the porch and immediately the animals rushed him, a small furry army that defied all logic.

They were organized.

He raised the shotgun and emptied two shells of birdshot into the onslaught. The spray effectively cleared the path but didn't—couldn't—stop them all. Birds were pecking at his hair and face. Squirrels and gophers were gnawing on his jacket and chinos. He beat them back the best he could, but he knew if he stood still they would peck and gnaw him to death. Two more shots filled the woods with fur, feathers, blood, and gun smoke. Aleksey wasn't fairing any better, holding the girl over his shoulder with one hand and shooting into the crowd of rabid creatures with his Ruger 9mm. The gun did nothing but make noise, no help at all. Squirrels and chipmunks were attacking the big man's legs and exposed arms, shredding layers of skin with tiny razor sharp teeth. The animals were overwhelming both men, but made no attempt to hurt the girl. Micah noticed that too and made use of it. He fired the shotgun again and again causing the animals to scatter and pushed Aleksey toward the car. They used the wrapped up captive as a human shield. Aleksey opened the back passenger-side door and tossed the girl in like a load of laundry. Him and Micah dove in next and slammed the door shut. A few of the creatures still connected to the men by their teeth and claws made it in the car, but the men made short work of them, crushing little skulls and snapping tiny necks. A fox managed to get a hold of Micah's ear and had torn most of it off. Blood flowed from a hundred small scratches and bite wounds. Micah climbed into the driver's seat and Aleksey stayed in the back next to the girl propped up against the window. The animals outside the car continued to bombard it like little kamikaze pilots. The wet smacking sound of them hitting the car's frame and windows was nerve wracking and Micah wanted to scream. It was madness.

"Drive, man, drive!" Aleksey yelled.

"I'm trying, goddammit!" Micah fished the keys out of his jacket pocket with shaking blood soaked hands. After several attempts, the engine finally roared to life. Over the sound of the engine and dying animals, something else was getting louder in Micah's ruined ear.

"What the fuck is that noise?"

"It is her." Aleksey answered.

"What do you mean it's her?"

"I think she is singing."

She was. Through the gag and under that sheet, the girl was singing. An unnerving falsetto began to fill Micah's brain. He punched the gas. The Oldsmobile plowed over a dirt road filled with hundreds of tiny living and dead bodies. The sound of crunching bones and high-pitched inhuman screams joined the melody coming from the back seat.

"Can't you shut that bitch up?"

"What do you want me to do? Krolowa was very clear we were not to damage her."

"I know that," Micah said, "but do something, pull the gag tighter or something. I know it sounds crazy, but I think she's causing this."

"Yes, I think that sounds crazy."

"Just do it!"

"Listen to me little one," Aleksey leaned into where the girl's ear should be and whispered, "I'm not supposed to hurt you, and I won't if you stop that noise your making. If you don't, I'll crush your throat like a soda can and take chances with bosses." He put his over-sized scratched up hand around the girl's neck and squeezed lightly for effect.

The singing stopped.

The animals suddenly stopped hurling themselves at the car and the birds stopped dive-bombing the windshield. The dirt path in front of the car began to clear as the woodland creatures began to scurry off back into the woods. As the road slowly cleared, only one obstacle remained.

Micah stopped the car.

"What the hell is that?" he said. He strained his eyes and turned on the wipers to clear the blood and broken birds from the windshield. Something sat in the middle of the road. *A dog*, he thought, maybe a huge bulldog. No, not a bulldog—a bull*frog*. It was a gigantic frog. The damn thing was as big as a tree stump. It sat in the dirt as if calling the men to task. The scene played like a bizarre old west showdown.

"Do you see that?" Micah asked his partner. "Is that a goddamn frog? It must be a hundred pounds easy."

"I don't care if it's a five-hundred pound gorilla, get us out of here, now!" Micah stomped the gas and blasted toward the frog. On cue, the frog's powerful back legs boosted the huge green amphibian into the air, catapulting it directly into the Oldsmobile's windshield with the force of a cinder block. Shattered glass, and a dirt-cloud of chaos followed. Micah lost control of the car and spun off the road directly into a tree. His neck snapped like a twig against the airbag and he died instantly. Aleksey was thrown through the shattered windshield and collided with the tree. Twenty-seven broken bones turned him into a leaking bag of red Jell-O on the forest floor. As the big man lay dying in the dirt, he heard blue birds begin to sing. He bled out in minutes.

*   *   *

Linen wrapped feet kicked open the back door of the smoking, wrecked car. The girl shuffled out of the wreckage and then out of the sheet she was wrapped in. Her hands had been free for hours, so she pulled the bandana off her mouth and untied her feet. When she was completely unbound, she did a little spin to puff out her baby blue taffeta dress and ran her fingers through her long curly red hair.

"Oh, I bet my hair is an awful mess." She said out loud.

"Ribbit." The rotund frog responded from his perch on the crumpled hood of the car.

The girl smiled, and spun again to face it.

"You know Renny," she said, " Sometimes I think the only reason you do that to yourself is for the kiss." She ever so daintily tiptoed over to the car, closed her eyes, and lightly placed a kiss on the bullfrog's slimy wet mouth. When she opened her eyes the frog had vanished, and in his place stood her oldest and dearest friend. A young man with a chiseled chin, who looked to be about twenty-two, stood naked and immediately covered himself to protect the girl's modesty. She turned her head away, but pointed to the trunk of the car where his limo driver clothes were stashed.

"Are you hurt Princess?" He asked as he slid into the black suit.

"No, but I'm tired, Renny. Take me home and contact *The Seven.* Tomorrow we seek revenge."

"As you wish, your highness, as you wish."

Taking Flesh

Chuck Regan

The word *Carnival* originates from the Latin *carne vale*, "Flesh, farewell."

> — *The Facts on File Encyclopedia of Word and Phrase*
> *Origins, 3rd Ed.*

Dan's brother Bobby was eating Cheerios at noon when he told us the carnival had set up in the middle of the night. We thought he was fucking with us. He fucked with us a lot, particularly me. Bobby said he thought they were cops at first with all the lights and how late it was—someone was always calling the cops on Bobby and his friends—but he said he stuck around and watched the carnies unload and get drunk. He said they had some real freaks working this year.

It was August, 1983. I was fourteen years old that summer, and a growth spurt had left me gawky and pimpled and a good six inches taller than the bullies who used to pick on me, leaving me with nothing to react to. It was the year I went into myself, and Dan, my best friend since First Grade, had been trying on his tough-guy persona. The next month we'd be freshmen in high school, and I was scared to death, but I wouldn't admit that to Dan, and certainly not to Bobby. Bobby, the soon-to-be-senior, told us stories about how the 'big kids' locked freshmen onto the roof, stole their clothes out of the locker room, and burned them with cigarettes and beat up anyone they felt like.

Bobby had taken every opportunity to terrify us with the details of what we should expect. I didn't have an older brother to tell me what it was really going to be like, and the more scared I got, the more short-tempered Dan had become with me. He had been spending a lot of time with kids he used to hate—the younger siblings of Bobby's friends, and I was surprised when Dan said he wanted to go to the carnival with me. It seemed like such a *little kid* thing to do.

"It's a different crew," Bobby said before going back to his room. "…after what happened to those kids last year."

I had heard the stories. Three kids got killed last year. We got on our bikes to go check it out.

*   *   *

As soon as we rode over the top of the hill, a bright red Ferris wheel broke the familiar tree line of the woods we had played in all summer. We sped down to get close.

All the machines were quiet. Wooden wedges were jammed against the tires. Painted-on grinning clowns and snarling animals glowered at us—their faces chipped and streaked with oil and rust. A chain clanked against an aluminum pole in a steady rhythm, stirred by a cool breeze blowing across the neighboring soccer field, carrying the smell of diesel and stale cigarettes. Nobody was around.

"Bobby had sex for the first time at a carnival," Dan said, dropping his kickstand.

Not knowing how to respond to this information, I just said, "Really?"

"Yeah. Behind the funhouse. He was thirteen, and she was a junior in high school," Dan said with pride.

We walked past the empty ticket booth, and my bowels gurgled. I laughed, but Dan ignored me. We circled the parking lot, looking at all the machines until there was nothing more to see. I turned to ask Dan if he was ready to leave, but he had walked off. I got a creepy feeling like he had been kidnapped by the carnies, but I found him standing, looking up at one ride.

"It was this one," Dan said.

The *Salt and Pepper Shaker*—two long, blue arms with licks of fire painted down the sides. Two caged baskets were ready to grab handfuls of screaming children and swing them into the sky.

"A screw came loose and the cage flew off. It crashed over there."

Dan pointed to a pile of old splintered bleachers overgrown with weeds.

"They put those there to cover up the blood stains."

*   *   *

Bobby had put a bug up Dan's ass that it was his turn to get laid, like he'd be disowned if he didn't accomplish this rite of passage before he got to high school. But Dan was doughy and weak-chinned, and I was scrawny and pimply and socially inept. Neither of us had had any luck with girls so far, so I knew we needed a plan if we were going to have any kind of shot at finding girls willing to deflower us.

The previous year, I had taken a summer class in photography and knew enough about my father's vintage Rangefinder 35-millimeter camera to load the film and focus it. The plan was to pretend to be working for the school newspaper and lure in some girls by appearing important. That night, I dressed in what I thought were my coolest clothes, and slung the camera around my shoulder like it was a rifle and rode my bike to the high school.

Dan met me at the far end of the soccer field. His hair was slicked back, and he was wearing his brother's old leather jacket. He looked ridiculous, but I looked even more awkward standing next to him in my outdated jeans and a Van Halen t-shirt I had never worn before.

"Let's do this," sounding like he was leading the A-Team as he pulled a plastic wrapper out of his pocket. It looked like an oversized Lifesaver candy. I nodded, but had no idea at the time what a condom looked like in a wrapper.

The carnival was already filled with bodies and the sun was still up. I saw girls from my classes, and some out-of-town girls that looked dangerous and delicious. I rated each of them in my head, but was too nervous to raise the camera to them. Dan tried to get me warmed up, pointing out scenes for me to photograph. Every time he raised his hands to frame his fingers into 'L's, the leather sleeves of his jacket creaked like an old chair. It was a cool night for August but he was sweating, and I was laughing. He told me to shut up and be serious.

He pulled me to the cotton candy vendor, where three girls in bright pink shorts were standing, eating mounds of spun blue sugar.

"Hey, girls, how about a shot for the paper?" he said. Slick.

They sneered, called us little pervs, and laughed as they walked away. Dan face got red as he watched them go. His nose dripped sweat.

"This is bullshit." Dan said, taking off the jacket.

"Let's do the bumper cars," I said.

"Fuck off. Leave me alone," he said.

I stood in the middle of the squall of lights and colors and cotton candy and sweat and watched him walk away. I should have been angry, I guess. For as long as I've known him, he had never talked to me like that.

Just as I was about to run after him, a man started hollering in a loud, angry voice. I heard a slap and a grunt and then a girl shrieked *Stop!*. Two grown men were fighting over a stuffed Garfield doll at the water gun booth. Snarls of rage pinched at their lips, glaring their cold eyes at each other, fists flying and hands grabbing shirts. I raised my camera.

Click.

Kids and adults pushed past me to get a clearer view of the fight. Two women with cut-off sweatshirts nudged into view. Their faces peeled into feral glee as blood bloomed at the corner of the one man's mouth. I advanced the film and took aim at the girls' expressions.

Click.

The stink of BO and funnel cake washed past me as two cops raced in to break it up.

Click.

The crowd booed and threw bits of caramel corn at the cops as they pulled the two men away. As the crowd parted, a carny—gaps in his teeth, bags under his eyes, hint of a skull tattoo under his shirt sleeve, dark, dandruffy, matted, and unwashed hair, grinned as he watched them go.

Then, he smiled at me like I was the only one there. The strobing lights made the shadows on his face dance. I raised my camera.

Click.

Like some drug was pumping out of the machines, I felt a hunger—not for food, but for something much deeper. I wanted more fights. I wanted to capture every sweat-clinging skirt and grimace of effort at the game booths. I rode the rides just to frame faces rippling with terror and elation as they flew through the night, strapped into deathtraps. I was caught up in a storm of flashing lights, the stink of fried food, and fear. I was just a ghost. Nobody seemed to notice me.

When I advanced the film and felt the tug at the end of the roll, a chill run up my back.

I had only brought one roll with me, and now it was over. I had been expelled from heaven.

*   *   *

During my sophomore year at college, I interned with Gerald Eiger—a wedding photographer. He seemed at first apologetic for exposing me to his world of complimentary drinks and Vaseline-smeared lenses. I guess he could sense that I thought I was better than him. I was just an asshole kid with a scholarship and a decent eye for composition. After I got the stick out of my ass, I learned a lot from him.

Gerry was a master at working with available light to frame a shot or to chisel a subject out of shadow. He instinctively knew the best locations for the obligatory shots—the cake, the dress, the ringed fingers—and how to work the aperture to turn the ugliest wallpaper or cheap plastic shrubs into mysterious, ethereal backgrounds.

On my first wedding shoot at a Veteran's Club, he assigned me the candid shots. I stood back from the smiling crowds and aimed at the people I thought were most likely to crack their facade of civility. My theme was to expose the secret meanings of the rituals of marriage. I wanted to capture the worried looks of the soon-to-be mothers-in-law, the proud and jealous glances of the bridesmaids, and at the reception, the 60-year-old aunts dirty dancing and leering like they were eighteen, and the teenaged nephews drunk off of abandoned champagne.

Back at his studio, after my rolls were developed, Gerry told me to stop thinking like an anthropologist and more like a game show host. He insisted that our job was to capture the illusion of marriage, not the reality. The clients wanted to see what they thought love was supposed to look like—misty roses and eternal smiles. He told me that they would discover the truth on their own soon enough. Let them have their illusions while they could.

I kept doing what I wanted to do. He smiled, shook his head and told me that I was just wasting film. People don't want to know themselves. They want to see what they expect to see.

"But I want to wake them up!" I said.

"Let 'em sleep."

*   *   *

After I earned my degree, I got a job at a local newspaper—photographing high school sports, teen pageants, and events at the mall. I kept telling myself that if I traveled to different assignments, I would eventually discover subject matter worthy of a project—a thesis to focus on, a truth to reveal.

I submitted what I thought was my best work to competitions. I received just enough recognition to compel my ego to keep going. I knew I was going to hit the big time eventually. I wrote off my overwhelming lack of success on the stupidity of the judges. They just didn't understand what I was saying.

After two years of nothing to add to my portfolio, no awards to brag about, and no decent meals to put on my table, I started doing weddings. Gerry was right—my analytical candids were always rejected by clients. They only wanted the faerie tale shots. I threw my best candids into a shoebox and gave notice at the paper. I committed myself to being mediocre, but with a fully stocked fridge.

Weddings required more labor than I had anticipated. Between assembling the books and promoting the business, I found myself reciting Gerry's same placating mantra: "At least I'm working in my field," as I sat holding a glue gun and glitter at a night school scrapbooking class.

I had earned my way into Hell, and whimsical stickers and corn husk raffia were the only coins I had to offer to the ferryman.

*   *   *

My last assignment with the paper was to photograph a sculptress in her studio. Her only claim to fame was that a large piece of hers had been installed in the courtyard of a newly constructed corporate center. The blocky, oppressive buildings were expected to enliven a small suburban town's economy, and anyone involved in the project was deemed newsworthy by the paper's editors.

I drove to the site and photographed the sculpture. The iron rebar-and-bronze thing was vaguely orb-shaped, with chrome tubes weaving in and out of its surface like a time-lapse photo of air traffic taking off and landing on a ruined Earth. I didn't understand what it was supposed to represent, and I judged the hell out of the *artist* as being a talentless hack who just fumbled out any nonsense her hands could throw together.

The world was upside down when *true artists* were relegated to crap jobs and hacks like this woman got big commissions to spew out bullshit like this orb-thing. Some idiot in a suit, his tie too tight, cutting off all circulation to his brain, decided that because he didn't understand the sculpture, it must be profound, and it had to be purchased. Soon enough, business-casual drones would be eating lunch under this thing's shadow, and my career would be rotting in obscurity.

I used a little of Gerry's techniques to bring out the textures, but the buildings were important to the context of the story, so I framed a few compositions—click, click, click— *documentation*.

I arrived late to the sculptress's studio. The reporter writing the story had already left, and the artist was eager to continue work on her latest project. I apologized for being late. Her hands were covered in clay and she apologized for not shaking my hand. In the middle of the garage studio was an oversized Gumby-like fern-arch-thing she intended to cast in bronze—a commission for a bank. She seemed in a daze as she told me to photograph whatever I wanted. As I looked around, she worked the clay, unenthusiastic, yet committed to the task—as if she were monotonously feeding a monstrous toddler gaping with bottomless hunger. My jealously for her success began to shift. She seemed trapped in her role.

Her hands moved in a meditation, slow and deliberately applying globs of clay—the final shape of the thing was some kind of inevitability that would be revealed to her. She had no control over it. She was merely fulfilling the role of a factory worker assembling parts designed by some other entity—some dark deity hiding deep inside her subconscious.

I learned something profound there in that studio. The artist, whose name I forget, had found the means for perpetual expression—one project paying her living expenses until the next project. She was living every artist's dream, but she seemed bored— imprisoned, like Gerry, like me. Her attitude toward her craft fascinated me. She was no longer struggling to prove herself to herself, and the money kept coming in. Her patrons demanded she produce more of whatever it was she had to say. I wondered if she had anything left to say, or if she was dried up like the kitschy scarecrow in her neglected garden.

I stayed for almost an hour snapping pictures. I didn't bother her with conversation, and she didn't seem affected by my presence at all. Her paint-spattered boom box, peppered with scorch marks, scraped out rambling late 70s prog rock as I lurked through her studio. Scribbled notes and crumpled sketches formed a nest woven with grocery lists and to-do lists—the exposed mind of a well-fed artist.

The sun dipped lower. The light crawled in through the big windows and onto her earth-clotted hands, burning there, providing a contrast on her smooth puckered flesh to a shadow on the sharp volcanic textures of the clay. *Where does the artist end and the art begin?*

The photos that came out of that session were the best I had taken since that night at the carnival when I was 14. I submitted the batch to a national arts magazine and they were enthusiastically accepted. The feature photo in my submission was the close up of her hands—her weedy, cinderblock garden providing Gerry-techniqued backlighting. To me, the shot perfectly expressed the melancholy of an artist's isolation.

There was no bigger thrill than seeing my work published. When I received my comp copy of the arts magazine, I drank a bottle of pinot noir in celebration.

I dreamt of the carnival that night.

*   *   *

I've had the same dream for twenty years: I am 14 years old, snapping photos of a carousel. Gold, cream, and blue antique horses waltz around a gaudy calliope as it brays vaudevillian dirges.

When I stop to load another roll of film, I drop my lens cap and it rolls under the ride. I duck down under the guard rail to retrieve the cap but I am pulled back by rough hands. The skull-tattoo carny from the photo breathes a rotted-teeth-and-cigarette breath onto my face and says, "You don't belong here." His words resonate nasally with a marshmallow hollowness. In recent replays of the dream, I have come to suspect that he has a cleft palate.

His calloused palm scratches my arm as he pulls me toward the house of mirrors then pushes me in. Actually, no. Every time I've had the dream, I just appear inside. There is no door I pass through. I've had the dream so many times, I usually realize at this point that I am dreaming and walk through the rest of it, waiting for it to end. That particular night, I wondered if the mirrors were supposed to represent all the photographs I've taken—distorted representations of myself.

I shuffle my way around the mirrors, kicking aside paper cups, avoiding the cotton candy cones stuck to the dusty plywood floorboards. The deeper I go, the thicker the dust gets until it is a dirt floor, and the litter is replaced by broken pottery and bones half buried inside a natural cave.

The passage narrows and I have to crawl. I scrape my elbows and knuckles and wonder if I will wake up with scabs. The cave opens up to a cold, empty darkness. There are primitive drawings on the walls. I try to study the drawings—I know they are important. It is always at this point that I wake up.

There are parts of the dream that change. Sometimes, I find a door to my parents' basement, and once or twice there was a washing machine or a set of shelves with my old toys on it. The carny's face is always the same. I can never remember the specifics of what is drawn on the cave walls, but every morning after I have that dream, I feel the urge to find a carnival. I fantasize that some state fair somewhere nearby has the door I need to find into this House of Mirrors.

That pinot noir hangover morning after the dream, I had just sit down to do a search for a local carnival when Todd my booking agent called me with a last-minute gig. A 75th wedding anniversary party. I refused the job. I lied and told him I had a conflict. I had no plans, but I had to do something else. If it wouldn't be a carousel, I would photograph an old bridge, or an automotive graveyard. I needed to find something, *anything* other than photographing the lies of smiling people.

*　　*　　*

In suburban Eastern Pennsylvania, carnivals exist, but they are too bright, too clean, too sterile. Neutered. Maybe it was because the rides were set up on the campuses of a Christian school or on church grounds, or the rides are too freshly painted—the kids are too happy. Something was radically different in those carnivals from that one I remembered. There was no danger present—no seething sexuality. Even after the sun had set, these carnivals never transformed beyond bland, clip-art caricatures. I deleted all but a few mediocre pictures on my digital camera. Wasted trips, I missed four weddings, and overdrew my bank account twice.

I fought off the toxic shininess of the winter holidays as if it were cancer, taking regular chemo treatments of scotch and bourbon. I sneered at the sight of each Nativity, each rosy-cheeked Santa, and every candy-light-decorated porch even while I photographed them. I still had to make a living. I submit to stock photography websites— royalty checks randomly fell into my PayPal account like coins from the sky.

First, I always make sure nobody is home. I carry model release forms with me in case I get confronted and have to ask permission to use the photos, but negotiating licensing is a pain in the ass, and a waste of time, and a potential bleed on what little money I make. This time, someone was home, but I couldn't resist. I climbed onto their front porch and used Gerry's lighting techniques, pulling my focus onto interesting details of lights and snow-dusted fir tree fronds. I clicked off a few shots that would make good schmaltzy greeting card covers, but every chirp of my digital camera only confirmed that I was no longer able to transport myself inside of that little framing window where I had been safely trapped that night at the carnival.

Of course, I had tried many times to expand my technique. An artist's expression is influenced by many things, including the tools he uses. I had switched to a digital medium almost a decade ago, but I occasionally experimented with old cameras—Polaroids and box cameras until the film was no longer produced. I used infrared film, warping lenses, filters, and digital filters—but each photo I took with those gimmicks turned out to look painfully self-conscious, like something a student would produce hoping their new tools would do the work for them. No matter what I tried, I confirmed to myself I was a fraud.

Every shot that came out of those sessions confirmed that I was a fraud. When the owners opened their front door, I thanked them for kicking me off their property. I was done pretending to be something I wasn't.

*   *   *

I resumed my search for carnivals at the first signs of spring. In late March, I found one in Maryland. I dug out my old Canon A-1 from the back of my closet and dug out a box of Kodak Tri-X black-and-white film from cold storage—the film had a nice grain to it, and great contrast in low light. If I was a fraud, this film would confirm it—it told no lies, only enhanced what I was exposing it to. I threw some road snacks and a thermos of coffee into the car and took off.

I had driven through an hour of rain after an unseasonably hot afternoon, and when I pulled into the parking lot of the sleeping carnival, the dusky sun was struggling to burn its way through storm clouds, a thin mist writhing on the ground. The gates were wide open but rides were dark, the kiosks open for business, but nobody inside them, like everyone had been snatched away. Full soggy trashcans reeked of spoiled meat and day-old vomit. The place had a dirty, hurried-taboo-sex feeling to it. It was perfect.

The rain had cast everything in deep contrasts. Shadowed surfaces were black mirrors that warped the world around them. The water drops clinging to every edge chimed with golden light.

Happy elephants were anchored to the legs of a bright red robot spider. Dead grey lights were planted in rows along its spiral limbs, like eyes of some primordial creature threatening to open. I switched to my macro lens and got in tight on one of the fiberglass elephants hastily airbrushed in grey and pink. A scar—a dead-fish-colored fibrous chunk was taken out of its trunk. Click. Pistons dripping pneumatic fluid were framed in the shadow of a hippo head. Click. The sign *Jumbo Whirl* was painted in cotton candy colors, encircled by light bulbs arranged in a dance of dead glass reflecting the milk-clouded sky. Click.

I stepped back and tried to remember how it felt to be a child, climbing aboard my first ride. These beasts were nothing like the buzzing ponies or shimmying helicopters stationed outside of grocery stores. As big as a small car, the beasts would push tiny bodies around in ways no child could be accustomed, rising higher than any tree they had ever climbed, spinning in circles designed to disorient. I wondered how many children had been initiated by this ride, and how many had puked on the seats. Still, the elephants and hippos smiled. Click.

I moved on to the *Ring of Fire*, a five-story vertical black hoop painted with flames—an alien hot rod prepped for takeoff. Or maybe it was an astronomical marker erected by ancient aliens. Fractured by the tree line, the sun peeked through the ring, shining a sharp, golden crescent on its center rail.

Each click of the shutter pulled me in deeper. Tighter compositions. Deeper contrasts. Sharper focus on the grime-crusted details.

The mystic morphine that drives every artist and athlete was rushing through me. I hadn't had to hand-return a roll of film for years, and I actually felt fear—fear that I wouldn't be able to get back inside that framing window, into that zone, but when I advanced past the last frame and felt it pull taut at the end of the spool, I knew my hunger was back. It had been such a long time since I had been that deep inside of that tiny window, I had forgotten how time can distort. The sun was gone, and so was my contrast.

I grinned like a madman as I spun the tiny lever on the camera, listening to the plastic clatter as tiny teeth pulled the exposed film back into its black shell. A drunken nostalgic thrill welled up in me. When the roll spun freely inside the camera, I felt as though I had retrieved a dream. I took out the roll and patted it in my pocket as if it were an engagement ring, then loaded the next roll.

I had been so caught up in my bliss, before I finished the next roll, I was shocked to see people stepping into my line of sight. The carnies had opened their games and prepped the rides as I had been traveling through some parallel dimension. The mist was long gone, banished by the hard tinny speakers blaring twenty year old rock music. Animated lights blinked anemically in the fading light. The rides began to spin, and as if lured in by their movement, people arrived.

*   *   *

Stuffed animals clutched in their grip, children swaggered through the crowds displaying the trophies they had killed with darts, ping pong balls, or water pistols. Teens ranging from lanky twigs to fully-blossomed proto-adults crowded around the booths. Boys masked in painted-on smugness demonstrated their impending manhood to every female within range as they hunted plush prey.

And there it was:

A gawky boy, about fourteen years old, bent over to throw a ring onto a bottle—a fierce concentration burned in his eyes. Three girls his age stood in the background. The one farthest from him looked past her friends at the boy. She licked an ice cream cone as her hair draped coquettishly over half her face.

Here were ancient fertility rites. Here was a proving ground for hunters—an otherworldly spectacle of lights and sound designed to bring forth a shift in consciousness—one that has been part of the human condition since before the written word. Here was our contemporary Stonehenge—a garishly lit circle made out of aluminum and chipped paint. The sacrifices were not in blood, but of money and ego, but the rituals were the same.

Spinning in circles the participants couldn't control, fear and a distortion of reality assaulted them. The games of chance were a reinforcement of that distortion—a player knows he should be able to toss a ring onto a post, or knock over a small stack of cups with a baseball. These hunters are told that their reality is not be as solid as they had imagined—the carnies were all trickster-shamans, they humbled those who were not aware that their world was not solid.

*   *   *

I spent that spring and summer driving across the tri-state area. Each carnival pulled me further into understanding these old rituals. Each roll of film explored my thesis more deeply, *Carnival as Ritual Space*.

Click. An obese family—their sausage fingers gripping bags and cones stuffed with multicolored foods of spun sugar and fried meat. Clots stuck to their necks and faces and shirts, they are sacrificial beasts stuffed for the feast.

Click. A young woman on a tilt-a-whirl is clinging desperately to her boyfriend. Her hair is whipped into a frenzy and her eyes are closed as some otherworldly puppet master tugs at her body. A mix of ecstasy and fear curl around her mouth—an orgasmic smile.

Click. A carnie throws his head back as he bellows to announce the next game. A demonic gleam in his eye threatens the camera to not reveal his secrets.

*   *   *

For the next few months, I focused on finding an agent, approving the layout of a book, then publishing and promoting it. That next spring, the book's premiere sold less than three thousand copies nationwide. Angela my agent assured me that those numbers were good considering it was my first coffee table book—I *hate* that phrase—and especially good considering my subject matter appealed to a very specific niche. She said she expected steady sales from the 'daytimer' market—those customers who hung out in bookstores, reading and browsing. She said they would discover my book eventually and sales would pick up. Their friends would see my book in their friends' homes, and reviews would be posted online. It would happen for me, she said. She told me that she believed in me, and told me that I should, too.

I obsessively checked the reviews. The few that I could find were mildly enthusiastic, but sales continued to trickle in. There was no way the advance was going to sustain me for long, and the royalties from other sources were just barely buying the groceries. I decided to go through my contacts and dig up some freelance work. It was June, and there were always weddings that needed photographers. I gave Todd a call.

*   *   *

Late that next August, I had a burst in sales. By mid-September, five hundred copies had sold in one week.

"See?" my agent said.

"I told you it would happen for you. I had three calls from magazines asking for the rights to reprint the cover photo."

That night, I dreamt about the carnival again. This time, after I reached for the lens cap, the camera strap snagged on the carousel and I was sucked under it. I smacked my hand on the bedside table when I woke up, trying to claw my way out.

Todd called me about a wedding gig and I mentioned my spike in sales.

"Maybe it's because of that kid who died," Todd said.

"What kid?" I asked.

A teenage boy had died on a carnival ride in Maryland. I had to dig out the model-release form to confirm his name. It was the boy I had photographed at the ring toss. He was the cover photo to my book.

My thesis had proven itself true. The carnival was an active ritual space, and every ritual needs some kind of sacrifice. That boy on the cover became a sacrifice to the carnival, and my sales spiked because of it.

Angela called me later that week to schedule a book signing. She said demand for my book was exploding. She said I had finally made it. She wanted to know what my next project would be.

Lazarus, Come Forth

Gareth Spark

The pistol was hard at the back of his jeans and Greg wished he were a professional; they would have a holster at least. The pistol, an old Yugoslav CZ-99, held nine rounds and there was another clip in the breast pocket of his check shirt. Csilla had given him the gun the night before, after a night of dining and drink he'd paid for out of his dwindling Army pension. She'd stroked a finger across his drooping, corn-pale Officer's moustache, raised his lust as though raising a ghost, then cut him off again, turned the talk to business.

"You need more bullets than that," she drawled in her thick Hungarian accent, "then you're already dead."

"You know a lot about it?" he'd stammered, trying to hold her, hoping it would be one of those rare nights when she blessed him with the benediction of her body, hard and lithe and his when she got the things she wanted.

"I wasn't always a waitress," she said, "as you weren't always a fat, old man."

"You're cruel."

"No," she'd said, "I just see the real you, the man inside, the warrior you were; that's the man I want."

She had cut into his days, livid and dark as a fresh wound, six months back, a waitress in the strip club where he came to feel halfway like a man. Retirement, endless days of playing golf with other old men, sun, cigars, siestas and, always, too much drink had pushed him near enough into the grave. He'd hoped to impress her with his stories, but mainly they were the memories of friends, dressed up as his own. He had never been a mercenary; he'd left the Army and headed straight into the Costa del paralysis. He hadn't so much as held a gun since retiring, in spite of what he'd told her over an intense, boozy week.

He nearly turned again to walk back. Now the car had broken down and the whole thing felt doomed. Crop trees of olive and lemon grew wild and ragged on the arid banks behind. He dragged a bandana from his pocket, wiped his face. It was hot and his chest was tight. Sweat dribbled through the wrinkles of his neck and soaked the collar of his shirt. *The bloody car*, he thought, *of all the things you didn't check.* It was a cheap second hand Datsun, and not for the first time, the relentless penury into which he had fallen, had made him into a fool. *You're an old fat man*, he thought, near enough 60, head turned by yet another pretty girl. He thought of her and pushed onwards, but there was a tremble in the animal part of his brain, and a shadow seemed to rise at the edge of his vision, a darkness flickering against the harsh sunlight.

Heat stained the sky where it touched the horizon and the breeze was dry and harsh against his sweating face. He felt grimy. A Toyota sped by, sounding its horn and Greg nearly stumbled into a ditch beside the cracked tar highway. Keep your shit together, he thought. The club was ahead on the left; about a hundred yards back from the road, almost hidden behind a thicket of diseased looking scrub; its warped plastic signs looked a hundred years old, Club de Banda, Sala de Massatge.

*   *   *

Csilla used to work for Nagy, the small-time gangster from Budapest who owned this place. He used to run weapons from the east for the cowboys of the euro zone, until he hit upon a better way to make money.

"Girls bring 20,000 a time," she had told him one night. "He finds them in Riga, Vilnius, Kiev, wherever, promises them work picking strawberries or something. Gets them here, and the men in the club tell the girls they owe thousands, the cost for bringing them.

They rape the girls, string them out on smack, force them to whore themselves to pay the debt. They say they have paid off the Police. It all starts with that bastard."

She'd heard he was back in Spain from the Romanian owner of the club where she worked and where Greg first met her. Greg didn't believe a word of it, but he needed her and he needed money; he could work a pistol and was desperate enough to do anything she asked.

He dragged a bandana from his pocket, wiped his face. Music played inside the club; he felt the bass thump up through the compacted stone of the ground. A door opened and a man came out of the club, wiping his face with the sleeve of his shirt. He was short and though young, almost completely bald. Greg watched him walk to a bike parked beneath a brown oak on the far side of the forecourt. The man was smiling until he noticed Greg. He pulled something held in a plastic bag from a satchel on the bike and walked across. "You're fucking late," he barked. "Where the hell have you been?" He was Irish, and the accent lay thick across his words.

"Sorry Declan, it was the car...."

"Save it . . . come on."

Greg felt the weight of the gun tug at the back of his waistband. *Keep your shit together; you've been in worse places.* He saw an endless highway of burning vehicles a world and twenty years away; the road to Basra, when he'd been a better and a younger man; somebody worth a spit.

Declan wiped his mouth. "You know your part?"

"I know it."

"You'd better, sonny Jim, because I'm not ending my days in a shithole like this 'cause some English tosser loses his fuckin' cool; that clear or not?"

"Clear."

"I told her not to fuckin' bring you in, told her you were just another old fat Brit with too many bullshit stories; a sad old relic, a fuckin' has-been, you never fooled me with your S.A.S. bollocks, man. I've seen the real thing at work, don't forget." He glared at Greg and something wild and electric danced behind his gaze like caged lightning. "Fuckin' Brits; come the fuck on then, and do your part right, Mister captain of the fuckin' guards."

Greg walked towards the black steel door and pulled it open. It was heavy, and he was assailed by a miasma of cigarette smoke, rank sweat, stale drinks and cheap perfume; there was a strong stench of burning wires too, probably power cables overheating; a cheap job. His eyes streamed and he wiped them with his thumbs as the door closed behind. Dance music played so loud that Greg felt it shake in his teeth. Men danced with empty-eyed girls whose bones poked against pallid bruised skin. Their eyes were luminous with hunger and narcotics; one had a distended stomach that showed against a stretched Lycra dress, and another"s eyes kept dipping closed as she rested her head against a man's shoulder. A shaven-headed bouncer stood at the door, arms crossed.

The last girl was on stage at the back of the room. She was naked and her body was very white against a shimmering foil curtain.

There were bruises on her pale thighs and upper arms. Her dark hair hung loose. She glanced at Greg with black eyes as she worked her way around a pole that wobbled when she pulled it.

Declan nodded to him and headed to a table in the far corner where a half-drunk glass of lager waited. Greg walked to the bar and leaned across it. His head throbbed and he tasted metal in his dry throat as he scanned the bottles. When he lifted his hands from the bar top, they left behind pools of sweat. He glanced again at the bottles lined on glass shelves and called, "Hello?"The old man's voice leaking through his throat caught him off guard and he glanced at the mirror in front. His thinning sandy hair was dirty and his eyes were hungry and red as rust in the half-light. He saw the young officer he had been, respected, obeyed, feared; then that imaged faded back into the pear-shaped, lusty fool before him. *You should walk away,* he thought, *right now, things aren't that bad, get a job, make a little money in a better way. Find a woman your own age.* He closed his eyes. *I need her. I need to be the man she sees.* A man walked through the battered door at the end of the bar and whispered something to the bouncer. Greg looked him over. He was dressed in navy sweats and a wife-beater that was tight on a heavily tattooed torso, Serban, had to be, Nagy's right hand, a smiling killer and the club's head of security. Csilla had told Greg all about him; the way he beat on the girls and the way Serban *never* stopped there. Greg nodded, trying to imbue the gesture with a nonchalance he absolutely did not feel. Serban did not return the gesture. He walked behind the bar, grabbed a bottle of vodka and joined the bouncer at a table close to the blacked out windows. He glanced at Greg, whispered something to the other man, laughed and then swigged from the bottle. Both spoke in a language Greg could not place, but he guessed was Romanian. He closed his eyes and didn't notice Csilla when she walked into the bar. She came through the same door the men had, marked 'Private.' Greg opened his eyes and his first instinct was to smile; then, when thought caught up, his grin faded. She wore a black polo shirt and cargo shorts and had pulled her bottle-blonde hair into a tight ponytail. Her eyes were hummingbird blue and flickered from the men by the window to him and back. "You're late," she whispered, her tongue rolling round the words like barbed wire.

"The car broke down, the heat I think...walking five miles through the Spanish summer isn't something I'd recommend, not for a man of my age at least, but then—"

"You're chattering," she said, "keep a hold of your nerves. I thought you were cool."

"I am cool." He said, but the word was clumsy in his throat and he cringed, angry with himself. "Let's just do this."

She opened the hatch in the bar and walked behind. She was trying not to look at him and her movements were stiff and uncomfortable. "The money's all here," she said, so quietly beneath the music he doubted she had spoken at all until she said again, "The money's here."

"Did he recognize you?"

"Why should he? It was a lifetime ago, in another country."

"Now you get your payback."

She stared at him for what seemed a long time and then said, "Have a drink, my love; it'll calm your nerves."

"It wouldn't hurt."

Csilla poured a large scotch. He grabbed the glass, sank it in one. She poured another, watched as he drank. "He's out back, they just did the deal; he's counting the money, then he'll be gone like a rat. We have to do this now. If you'd been on time..." She let the word hang.

"Just the two chaps to my left, are there?"

"Yes," she said, "and they are enough, believe me."

Greg glanced over at the men. Serban sat with elbows on the table. He scanned the room with steady black eyes. The other leaned back, rolling a cigarette. His tongue stuck out as he concentrated on the task and the stubble across his scalp was dark and greasy in the dim light.

Csilla reached for a rag and swiped it at the zinc bar top distractedly. Her young face was harsh in the white light. "You have to do it now; Declan will cover the rest."

"I know."

"Now," she said.

Greg closed his eyes. His heart punched up at the base of his throat like something wanting out. "Say it for me; say it for me one more time."

"Szeretlek," she sighed, "I love you."

The girl who had danced on stage was suddenly beside Greg at the bar. Csilla, without asking, poured a glass of fizzy water and placed it before her. The girl drank it slowly, in sips, without a word, staring all the time into nothing.

"Help me." The girl's voice was slight beneath the thumping music.

Greg looked at her from the edge of his eye. "I'm sorry?"

She leaned closer and spoke softly, her lips hardly moving. "I believed them. I believed everything and look now."

Csilla glanced at the Romanians. Serban was on his feet, gaze fixed on the girl. "Greg," she said.

Greg asked the girl, "What's your name?"

"Sofia," she said. "You must help." She tugged his sleeve. "Please."

The Romanian grabbed her shoulder, yanked her backwards, and snarled something into her ear. She replied quickly in a high, choked out voice and the man raised a hand that was aching to cause some hurt. "Don't," Greg said. *Maybe it doesn't have to be about the money or the woman, maybe be the gentleman again, the knight glittering against the world's darkness, the man who'd walked into enemy fire more than once to save a young life; maybe this is the last good chance to come back from the shadows and burn.*

Serban turned and stared at him. "What?"

"I said don't."

In a sudden movement, quick and rolling as a flame through dry scrub, Serban threw the girl to the ground and grabbed Greg's shirt.

The pistol worked loose, clattered to the floor. Serban heard it, frowned. His friend yelled something and Greg heard the scrape of chair legs before his animal brain took charge. He rammed his forehead into the Romanian's face, broke cartilage. Serban stumbled, grabbing at his nose, instinct driving back his fight.

Greg dropped for the pistol.

He saw Declan, on his feet, saw the cut down barrels of a hunting gun, saw them spit flame and crack like thunder on a tin roof.

Greg lifted the pistol and shot the bouncer twice in the chest. He crumpled backwards into the table. Glass smashed and Greg felt wet heat against his skin. Touched a hand to his cheek and it came back crimson, gritty with shattered bone. A woman screamed. He heard Declan, "Don't none of you fuckers move a fuckin' finger, entiendo? Somebody shut that bitch up!" He heard the slam of a shotgun meeting bone; the sound cut through the thumping music as if a bundle of dried twigs cracking against a flame and the screaming stopped.

Greg stood. His hands trembled. He looked down at the mess that was the dancer; limbs crooked and swastika-splayed, grey bone and scalp and innards turned wet and purple against the neon. Declan's first shot had caught her. Blood ran from her throat like water from a squeezed sponge. Her hands grasped weakly at her ruined neck and he heard a sucking sound come from her chest. The dancer's eyes were wide, and he thought of a scared dog. Then the blood stopped along with her heart and her small hands cracked against the tile.

Csilla was rooting through the fallen Romanian's pockets. "Come on," she said, "Serban, you fool, where are they?" She looked over at Declan. "You, get those people into the corner; Greg, come with me."

"You heard the lady," Declan yelled. "All of ye's over in that fuckin' corner." He said, then repeated it in heavily accented Spanish and there was a clatter of shattered glass and discarded chairs as the men and girls moved over to the wall. He reloaded the shotgun and held it level, spoke to Csilla over his shoulder without looking. "We don't have all the fuckin' time in the world, sweet pea, now crack on! I'll wait here for ye."

It was hot in the corridor. The air was thick and heavy with the fragrance of flowers stood either end of the dark hall in high ceramic pots. To hide the smell, Greg realized, because it was there, beneath the detergent and flowers and perfume: the rank odor of the human animal.

"At the end," Csilla said.

Greg checked the chamber of the pistol. The door at the end was boxed hardboard, painted with a powdery white emulsion. He raised a chunky leg, felt a moment's hesitation, then plowed a British Army size 12 boot into it. It broke as if it were ice, with a thunderbolt crack. He felt alive then, powerful, a tiger woken from a decade's long slumber. He was the man he used to be - the berserker, the Captain who faced down a squad of Saddam's guards in the dust outside Basra. She had brought him back, a Lazarus with death in his hands.

Nagy appeared, blocking the doorway with his body, and then fell to his knees. He was a huge man, fat, bald, weeping into the collar of a track suit zipped up tight against his throat. Csilla looked down at him, her tired, kohl-stained eyes filled with a mixture of sorrow and contempt, a defiance that radiated from every part of her.

"So here you are." She spoke with a softness that surprised Greg, with a lilting eastern accent that was at once familiar and exotic.

Csilla pushed him back into the room. It was very small: a double bed, unmade; a small basin, a mirror above it; brightly colored bottles of shower gel and deodorant and other cleansers crammed onto a pine shelf; a full length mirror; all lit by a single bulb shining through a red fabric shade. The money lay on the bed.

"No," Nagy said, "It can't be you.""Greg, the money," she said. "Give me the gun."

Greg handed her the pistol as Nagy spoke quickly in Hungarian. Csilla smashed the weapon into his skull and knocked his fat body to the floor. He lay face down on the stained rug, weeping, as Greg scooped bundles of 100 Euro notes into a gym bag.

"That's all the money," he said, "we should go."

"At least you were good for something in the end, pig," Csilla said.

Nagy lifted himself up slowly, pleading. The shot was massive when it came, a break of summer thunder tearing through the room, deafening and final. Nagy fell as if he were a cow dropping to the slaughterhouse floor, the thud of meat against stone.

Csilla turned. Her eyes were very white against the blood spattered across her face. "Let's go," she said. Greg started back the way they had come. "No," she gestured with the pistol towards a door opposite, "this way."

"What about Declan?" They'd left the Irishman in the bar where he held the club's afternoon patrons; Greg heard him yelling threats all the way from downstairs. "Fuck him," Csilla said, "you cannot rely on a man like that, too twitchy."

"We're going to leave him? What if he talks?"

"You're kidding, right? When the Guardia Civil turn up, he'll fire first, it's his way. Then they'll fill him with a hundred bullets," she pulled the door open, "that's their way."

The sun was low now, burning in the sea on the far side of the plain where dust on the road to Tarragona rose in stuttering clouds. Greg gazed at the baked red of the country, his back turned on the concrete block of the brothel and said, "That's it now, babe; that's it from now until forever; we're going." He kissed the top of her head. "I love you Csilla." He kissed her again and this time she looked up into his face. Her eyes were red, as though rubbed with pepper. There were sirens in the distance. "Come on," he said, leaning in to her again; then the world crashed down. She had shot him in the gut. It burned a riot of pain like a rushing fire through his being and he buckled to his knees. The sirens, he heard the sirens. "You should have brought a car," she said. "I can't trust you not to fuck things up."

He fell to his side, clutching the hot wet stickiness of his life as it passed into the dust. She pushed the pistol into her waistband and lifted the satchel. Her face was grimy with blood and dirt. She rubbed her eyes and walked towards Serban's car beside the patchy undergrowth.

Greg gasped something as she climbed into the car. Then she said, almost to herself, "It was not to be."

The sirens were closer now and she tore the car out into the road, raising a shroud of brown dirt that hung in the air like a dirty fog. She headed south on the Cami de Reus, towards town, glancing at the evening sky and ignoring the rank, coppery smell of blood drying on her clothes.

The Roach Motel Reputation

Ryan Sayles

"One of you mother fuckers knows who and where this Thomas kid is and I'll give the entire bar to the count of five before I start staking people to the wall for not answering."

I say this, as honest as a priest telling a whore she should consider new work. I've been hired to locate this punk, Thomas. Rumor has it he haunts this rat's nest.

It's a little past one in the morning. I forget the day; here in our city any portion of the week at one AM is as dark and bleak as

Purgatory. Every night is just one endless stretch of fog, shades of gray, layers of shadow. A perpetual chill breathes through the urban decay. It finds its way inside your gut no matter how many shots of whiskey you guzzle to find warmth.

Inside this bar, squirming quietly, this maggot tier of humanity is trying to be tough as nails with me. But they know their soft underbelly shows through.

The bar is aptly named *Hidden*. The sign above the front door facing the street reads *BAR*. Nothing else. Only those who frequent the joint know its given name. It's owned and operated by two men who are card-carrying members of *NAMBLA,* the North American Man/Boy Love Association. Filing this wretched hive are equal numbers molesters, rapists and more molesters.

There are two ways into this place: the front door and the back door. The mouth and the asshole. The mouth is shut behind me and the asshole is on the other side of all these deviants. It dumps out into the trash-littered alley behind the bar. Lined with drunk bums and overflowing waste cans, the alley is little more than the toilet this bar squats in front of.

I have a pretty solid hunch I'm the first man to walk through that entrance who has a fighting chance of not going straight to Hell. Damnation is formed by certain actions here on earth and this bar welcomes them all. The crowd in here is small; their kind rarely likes to leave the gutters.

I stand here, shrouded in pools of darkness as lacy and fickle as smoke; a silhouette of a linebacker-sized man in his fifties dressed in a trench coat that is loosely tied in a way that any experienced eye will tell you is ready for a quick draw. The bar is tense the way the air is before a tornado. Not many dudes here tonight: easier to make good on my threat.

Because I will.

"Thomas? Come out come out wherever you are."

I walked inside and the place came to a standstill. I'm not one of their kind and they know it. They are downwind and can smell the predator on my fur. And since I won't go away the bar patrons just remain quiet, counting on the long, sinuous shadows in this tavern to mask them from me.

As if I'll just go away at some point. My fist squeezes around a set of brass knuckles, dented and chewed up from rubbing across teeth over the years.

"Fine." I say, a smirk warmly growing across my lips. "I'm sure all of you had this coming anyway."

Yellow, hollow eyes turn to me. My statement casts a hushed silence. The reek of cigarette smoke, a mélange of fruity alcohols and the stench of this breed of abnormality lays thick in here.

"One." Warning. I step forward in the general direction of the perverts nearest me.

"Two." Cold. Now I hope no one speaks up.

Like any deviant bar; gay, biker, country, whatever, this tiny niche has sprung up and been filled by a watering hole. Of course it's as *hush-hush* as the truth in Hollywood that half its leading men are queers. I caught wind of it some time ago when one of my clients spilled its location and population. He hired me for some quick photography work; some clean black and white shots of a mark walking to and from here. The client paid me outright for the photos and never called again.

I'm pretty sure I did some PI work so the client could blackmail the mark. Oh well. Money spends the same. My license doesn't say anything about being picky.

If word got out that a bar centered on sexual predators existed-even here, south of the river in the Burrows-it would catch fire faster than a Scientologist in Hell. Tinderbox. And everyone inside it would be kindling.

And, if things don't go my way tonight it will be that anyways.

"Three." Determined.

"Who the fuck is this guy?" One of the child molesters asks the room. He seems fed up enough to pop his mouth off. He still won't make eye contact with me, but at least I'm finally seeing someone display some balls here.

The mouthy gentleman is really just some fat piece of shit sitting at the bar proper, trucker hat seated high on his brow, beer mug in his soft hand. By the velutinous but poisoned look of him he had to turn to children. No man or woman would be interested in him enough to trust their back to him.

Someone I don't recognize whispers to the room, an answer to the call. He says: "Richard Dean Buckner."

People know that name. *My* name.

Eyes express the recognition. And that's all I need. The entire crowd at the pool table collectively takes one huge step away from a goofball lining up his shot. They clear out so quick it's as if he farted AIDS.

Now we're talking. I light a smoke.

Read on the goofball: young. Not so young to think he's bulletproof, but not old enough to think he'll die from getting shot either. Care free and stupid by nature, hardened to a degree by his lifestyle. He wants to project an image like he's galvanized. It's in his eyes. But he's not. He wears his meekness on his sleeve like it was a embarrassingly cheap price tag. No hiding that.

Thomas looks at his supposed friends, back to me, back to them and then me. He realizes in a microsecond he is without quarter now. A naked fool in a house of razors. Vulnerable.

A confused mask of fear and anger scrawls along his face. It turns to resentment. All alone now. He stands up straighter, identified to his hunter by the herd of turncoats he was inside. It seems the whole strength in numbers thing falls apart when you are the one your numbers offer up as a sacrifice.

But then again, the underbelly here knows me in the city and no one wants their name on my lips. I got the roach motel reputation.

"Hello Thomas." I say, smile around my cigarette.

I stroll his way and the bar remains quiet, focused. Wondering if I am going to stay with this guy or simply *start* with him. Only time will tell.

My eyes seer his face. His eyes downcast; submissive. I spend more time watching his hands. Furtive movements. Just programming from the academy years ago. Another life, really.

Tells. They're all tells. And everyone has one.

And this sexual deviant, eyes downcast and submissive as I roll up to him, the entire bar watching to see our play, his face says weak but his hands are gripping the pool cue. Strong enough it seems. Strength borne from fury. This could get good.

He's been to the pen. Obvious. He's not going back. Obvious. I'm a little surprised I'm not getting the Felon Stare. Maybe he doesn't realize I don't have arrest powers anymore. Doesn't matter. In this day and age I wouldn't be able to haul him into Central Processing after the beating I'm planning on doling out. My days on the force passed away with the old school.

I've seen Thomas's kind before. Even cowards might bare their teeth when their back in is a corner. Whatever fight is in the kid should be easily dashed. Just enough force to establish dominance. Then the coward will resurface. Compliant.

"What's going on tonight?" I say, closing the gap.

"Tonight, sir?" He says. Games. Buying time. Dodging.

"Don't repeat. Answer."

"Well, just a little bit of FUCK YOU!" And he snaps the pool cue over a knee. Been to the pen. Not going back.

Jabs with the hilt. I swing with a right cross that would make Mike Tyson think twice about trying to eat me and the pervert sails over the pool table, a mid-air trail of blood following his face.

Maybe a little bit more force than needed to establish dominance. Oh well.

He collapses. I go around and take a handful of hair. Lift him up. Face-plant him on the table. The green felt is instantly soaked, ruined. Holding the back of his head, pressing so hard I can feel a loose tooth in the front of his jaw give way, I look up to the bartender.

"Get this place hopping again and stay out of our business before I draw my iron and clear the house."

The bartender, a man who would look right at home with a ball gag in his mouth and a strap-on pummeling him into ecstasy, he nods quickly. He makes eye contact with a few other freaks and all of a sudden the jukebox starts back up, murmurs grow out of silence, conversation grows out of murmurs, glasses clink, heads turn away.

Business as usual again.

I yank the deviant up from the reddish-brown, tacky felt. Soaked through already.

"We've got the table to ourselves." I say.

I think he's crying.

Good.

*   *   *

"Tell me about *Hypno Disco*." I say. I already know the answer.

A minute ago I let him up on his own two feet. Set another pool cue in his hand. I kept him on the opposite side of the table from the door. If he bolts, he's got to pass by me first.

Showed him my iron; six slugs of .44 magnum ready to chase his ass to the Great Beyond should he fuck this up.

"Set us up for 8 Ball." I said. "We'll talk while shoot."

He set us up. Now I want to know about *Hypno Disco*.

He stares at me for a moment; gauging. This isn't a new song and dance. He's trying to read me. See how little he can get away with by telling me. He's been to the pen, so the law has questioned him. He's a punk and probably always has been, so dad has questioned him. The big difference here, with me?

I'm not above breaking things for answers.

He considers hard, then looks away, maybe at the wall behind me, maybe at my collar, maybe at the tattoo on my neck, and shrugs. Begins in a nonchalant fashion. Like we're not talking about the three dead people all this leads to. "It's some roving rave party. Some guys I used to know hit it up all the time. I haven't made it out in—"

"Wrong."

He stares again, this time afraid.

"Trying to gauge me?" I ask. I get tired of this shit. "Trying to measure my reaction? Figure out how I'm one step ahead of you? How do I know you're lying right to my face? Try harder Pee-Wee, because you suck at reading people and this is going to cost you a serious ass beating."

His brow sheens with a slight layer of sweat. Called out. Pegged.

"You were dead wrong." My cue comes down across his fist, right on the knuckles. I figure I can either just snap one at a time, drawing attention as I torture this freak in front of his friends, or we can have one big learning session and get it over with.

He drops to his knees. Hand cradling the other. The struck knuckles swell twice their size in a split second. I walk over; get so close he can smell the oil on my gun.

"Get up and try it again. I'll go ahead and break."

He wobbles up to his feet, good hand supporting him on the table. I can see the tears shiver in his eyes. I lean, pump the cue a few times and strike the albino cue ball. Break the triangle. Sink two solids and one stripe.

"I tell you what, Thomas. I'll take the stripes." I light a smoke and ash on the floor. "You know, funny story. I played a guy once who thought that solids were the way to go in 8 Ball because he figured since both players were working towards the 8, whichever player was solids would have one less ball to sink and therefore had the advantage right off the bat."

Thomas just looks at me. His hand looks bad. I don't think he's physically able to play. Oh well.

"Tell me about *Hypno Disco.*"

Through his pain, words quivering: "Alright. I have some friends from the pen who operate a roving rave called that. They network with folks to find empty warehouses and shit. Keeps it moving around. Dodging pigs, you know. Hell, they used an old Naval Air station hanger once. They used the basement of some closed-down church."

I bank shot one ball into a corner pocket.

"They just needed to keep it moving. Usually run it twice a month. It was a good time." He says. "We just liked to get down. Party."

Harold Miller, age 68, white male retired from the Army, husband to Diane Miller, father of four, grandfather of nine, lived north of the river here in Saint Ansgar. One of his sons-in-law told me all of this. Guy by the name of Bradley.

Harold, apparently he had a hell of a time sleeping for years. Finally got prescribed some form of Benzodiazepine. Valium, Xanax, Halcyon, whatever. The brand name doesn't matter. It was just some slumber vitamin.

"Names." I say to Thomas. I catch one ball at a severe angle and use it to gently tap another into a side pocket.

Thomas wastes no time. "Willie the Deer and a guy named Shooter McGavin. Like from that Adam Sandler movie."

"Willie, huh?"

"Yeah. Willie the Deer. 'Cause he's hit four deer with his car. Dude just can't catch a break."

Willie, born William A. Hunt, is known to the police as 'Willie the Deer' because he was in a stolen car and got in a high-speed chase with three black and whites. Ditched them all. Then promptly hit a deer head-on and wrecked. He was caught that way, using the Jaws of Life to pull him from the ruined vehicle. Whatever bullshit he tells his friends is his business.

The car Thomas is alluding to is Willie's personal possession, an early '80s Mercury Grand Marquis. Ghetto-ed up with all the trimmings. Gold-spokes, low rider wheels and rims, window tinting ten shades darker than allowed by law, hydraulics, the whole nine yards.

"Tell me about your involvement with the rave."

"I'm the street guy. That's all. I do posters, hand out flyers, any kind of guerilla advertisement it needs. I start the phone tree to let people know the when and the where." This much is true; I've heard it before from someone else. There are other things I know he's leaving out.

But we'll get to that later.

Harold Miller was killed five weeks ago in a car wreck. No high speed chase, no deer. Family said he'd been acting very strangely for the past few days, maybe a week tops. Tremors, shouting, throwing things, small delusions like he left his keys on top of a piano they sold in 1986.

Then he has a day of clarity. All that bizarreness that had dominated his actions just *poof!* Up and gone. Back to normal. Bradley, Harold's son-in-law, said the family was worrying about dementia. They realized after the fact that the worry, the *new* worry of something *else* being wrong, something *worse* than Harold's sleeping problems, it paralyzed them into inaction. They just needed some time. And then this day of clarity comes along and they all breathe a sigh of relief and thank God that whole thing was over with.

It only took one day. Twenty-fours of acting *better* to throw them off guard that much.

So when Harold tells his wife he's going to the pharmacy, she thinks nothing of it. She's relieved. Everything is okay. A car trip means he's normal.

"Where is Willie now?" I ask. I already know the answer.

"Willie is probably with his girl. Her family owns a boat. Or he might be with that Latino chick he's fucking. Or he's out with Shooter."

Wrong.

I hit the cue ball, bank it off a side, get a good *thwack!* out of a stripe that zooms across the felt and hits two solids. Sinks them both. The stripe spins to a stop on the pocket's edge, jitters, refuses to sink. I eyeball it with a cold stare. It falls in.

Damn right.

Witnesses said Harold Miller was screaming inside his vehicle, said his face was a vehement mask of fury, swerving from side to side until he ran up a lane divider, into oncoming traffic, through an abandoned store front. The cinder block and poured-in concrete rear wall of the store stopped him. Dead. Face wrapped around the steering wheel.

"Word on the street is Willie sold drugs at the raves. What about that?" I already know the answer.

"Well, Willie would deal X. Party dope, really. We were just there for the gettin' down—"

"What put you in the pen?" A curve ball.

Thomas withdraws on the cellular level. It's written all over him like a tattoo of shame. Withering inward as a defensive mechanism. His guilty verdict is still very tender.

Thomas casts a sidelong glance and says: "Being gay. That's the only thing."

"Wrong."

My pool stick swings across his outer thigh like a lumberjack felling a tree. Drops him. The legs just go out. Flipping a switch. The nerve bundle in the thigh I just overloaded is sympathetic; hit one and both react. Like twins.

Thomas stands back up. He's got assistance from my .44 magnum. It's inside his mouth, lifting him as if he were a hooked fish.

"Try again. And stop acting like I don't already know."

The gun comes out, the barrel wet with saliva, he stammers, cradles his broken hand. He looks here and there. Then: "He was good looking, alright? Athletic. Charming. I was confused about me. This was years ago. I was confused. It's hard, man. Dad didn't take it well when I told him and mom. Dad was going to throw me out but mom stopped him. My older brother was weird around me. I have two sisters; one was giddy and always asked me to go shopping. The other stopped letting me hold her baby.

"And then the neighborhood kid was just coming down the street. It was a hot day. The neighborhood has a pool and the kid was swimming. Tanned there all summer. Good looking. Charming. I was drinking beer in my driveway and I hated myself. He stopped, we started bullshitting, I gave him a beer, he was a lightweight, he needed to lie down, we were drunk. I slept with the kid.

"But only because he said he was fine with it. I swear. I thought we... we had something. I don't know.

"His parents said it was rape. Dad agreed. Threw me under the bus. But the kid— the kid just wanted it over with and when he testified it was difficult but the jury thought it was consensual. I guess he was confused too. Maybe we *did* have something until other folks brought up the 'R' word and spoiled it.

"So I got tagged with providing alcohol to a minor and statutory rape. He was fourteen."

At the time of his death, a burnt-out physician was attending to Harold Miller. The Benzodiazepine family of drugs is the least effective and most dangerous with seniors. I think Bradley spoke with the ME. The ME knows the risks, and preformed a tox screen on the corpse.

Harold hadn't been taking his medications for a week.

"Tell me about *you* dealing on the rave floor." I say to Thomas, lighting a smoke and leaning in to clear the table of his solids.

"I—" Stops himself.

Now we're getting to the meat of it.

Tries again: "Sometimes Willie would want me to push some X. I'd just wander around, letting people know it was available if they wanted."

"Is that all?"

Emphatically: "*Yes. That's all.*"

"Really? Oh good." I set the pool cue down. Walk to him. "Then you can tell me about Susan and Madison. Explain that."

"Oh no—" His eyes well up with tears. His lip trembles like a fault line. Any fight that might have existed before slinks away; evaporates like hope with a gun pointed at it. A tell. The biggest. The only tell, really.

Any questions I did come here with are answered. The pieces fit together. I've got the story now.

I take my phone out and thumb a few buttons. Wait until the screen reads MESSAGE SENT and re-pocket it. I look at this guy, sneer.

"Outside, Thomas. Quiet like. Make a scene in here and the bodies will be on the news tomorrow night. Got me?"

He nods. We walk. We shed the bar behind us and the bitter night sends runners of frost up our nostrils and down our throats. Prickly, icy fingers worming their way into my coat, my sleeves and pants. One hand on my iron, he and I walk towards the car parked in the deepest pool of shadow I could find.

"Hey," he says, perking up. "There's Willie's car!"

"Is it?" I ask. I already know the answer.

"Yeah. Yeah!"

"Let's go say 'hi'."

Bradley the son-in-law called me out of the blue. Said I helped out the friend of a friend of a friend. Said he heard good things. Told me about Harold. Told me what he suspected about Thomas. Turns out Bradley has a solid head for such things.

Thomas disappeared weeks ago but Bradley remembers Willie's car. Willie had the logo of the custom body shop that does his work printed across his rear windshield. That lead me to the shop, the shop lead me to Willie, Willie told me about *Hidden*.

Just past Willie's car is another set of wheels. Unmarked, engine running. Graham Clevenger, detective sergeant of the Saint Ansgar PD standing beside it. An island in a sea of night. He was my old partner back when he was green and I was head detective in the city bureau.

Clevenger approaches. Eyeballs the kid. "Got the text." He says.

"Now are you glad you came with me?" I ask, one fist gripping Thomas's arm as tight as a gorilla. Clevenger followed me here tonight, waited in his ride while I did the dirty work.

"No." Clevenger looks past me to *Hidden*. "Not to this place."

I look to Thomas, whose face has become smeared with terror at what another man might mean to his situation here.

I drag deeply; let the smoke come out with my words: "So your dad doesn't like having a gay kid and you two co-exist with an ever increasing wedge in your relationship." I say, gun out. "Then he wrecks and dies, and they can find no trace of his medication in his system. The symptoms of sudden withdrawal from Benzodiazepines range from violence to comas. Delusions, mania, confusion, all that. Your dad starts exhibiting these behaviors and why?"

"No no no nonononono—"

"Why is because his kid pushes dope on his buddy's dance floor. His kid hates his daddy. His kid knows that a common party drug just happens to be what his dad takes. Maybe Willie was running light on X; maybe he just wanted to add to his illicit pharmacopeia. Maybe you wanted some money on the side. Maybe you wanted to get back at dad. I don't know. But *you* knew. So you steal your father's prescription, replace it with some placebo aspirin pill and start to deal. I found a flier, Thomas. Nine days before your father lost his mind, had a violent hallucination while driving and ran off the road you guys partied in a warehouse over on the dock."

"Oh God no nonono—"

"Did you think about the withdrawal? Did you care? Of course, how could you know that your father would take your older brother's two children along with him on his last ride? Huh? Susan and Madison? A stroll with Grandpa."

Thomas is crying now. Hard. Guilt has a particular sob that other tears don't.

"You just wanted to make some money off your queer-hating dad's back. Fuck 'em if he wants to endanger the lives of others, right?"

"I didn't mean for any of this—"

"Plows right through the store front. From the skids the investigators estimate forty-seven miles an hour. Travels thirty-six feet of retail space and crumples on the rear wall. In any wreck there are three impacts: car versus whatever it strikes, human inside the car versus the inside of the car, and the human's guts versus the internal walls of the body."

I lean in. "The ME said those girls were liquefied. *You* did that."

No response. Just sobs.

"C'mon, bud." Clevenger takes possession of him. Handcuffs. "You have the right to remain silent, you have—"

It goes on. My old partner seats the punk in the back of the unmarked and walks back over to me.

"Family hire?"

"Brother-in-law."

"Good to see you again."

"Thanks. I'll be over for Christmas dinner."

Clevenger raises an eyebrow. I look at it and say: "I'm invited, right?"

"I guess." He says.

"Good. Molly will be glad to hear you said that."

"All right. I'm taking this kid downtown. Thanks for the collar."

"Not a problem."

In the back of the unmarked, squirming inside the cage, Thomas is crying. Screaming he's sorry. He didn't mean it. If he could turn back time… if only this. If only that.

Apologies mean nothing to me. Especially from a rapist drug dealer with a chip on his shoulder who sets up a man to accidentally kill himself and two children.

Clevenger drives off. I walk back to Willie's car. Put out my smoke. Put on my gloves. Get in the driver's seat.

Willie, born William A. Hunt, is known to the police as a suspect in several chemically-assisted rapes. Party girls, waking up the next day with no recollection of the night before but with strong vaginal and anal sensations of sex. The police opened a file, ran down some leads, cross-referenced statements, et cetera. They all pointed back to these raves. The same ones that kept moving around, making it harder to track. Enough evidence and victim testimonies pointed to Willie as to perk ears.

Oddly enough Willie, Shooter McGavin and even Thomas here are hard to track down. Good thing I'm a great private detective.

When I found Willie, he smelled cop like a true rat. Tried throwing a haymaker. Failed. Tried getting a thumb in my eye. Failed. When he tried to bite my face I kneecapped him just to take the fight out of him. I always have to remind myself that kneecapping with a .44 magnum is overkill.

After Willie spilled the beans to me about where to look for Thomas, he bled out from the wounded leg. It's better than hitting a deer at sixty miles an hour. His body is cooling off, crumpled inside the truck of his four-wheeled pride and joy. We drive north for a few minutes, to the old and abandoned Navy pier. The lighting here is terrible, and conducive to surreptitious, nocturnal activities.

No one misses Willie as I roll the car into the river. Thomas will go down easy. Case closed.

It doesn't bring Susan or Madison back, but it puts the final period on a lot of other things. That's the trade off.

Now to use the rest of Bradley's retainer for whiskey. I'm pretty cold tonight.

(originally published in Crime Factory #7 under the pen name Derek Kelly)

About the Authors

Paul D. Brazill

Paul D. Brazill is the author of A Case Of Noir and Guns Of Brixton. He was born in England and lives in Poland. He has had writing published in various magazines and anthologies, including The Mammoth Books of Best British Crime 8,10 and 11. He has edited a few anthologies too, including the best-selling True Brit Grit – with Luca Veste. His blog is here.

Mark Krajnak

Photographer Mark Krajnak hails from Allentown, New Jersey. His work has appeared on album and book covers, including the upcoming *Trouble in the Heartland*, in *New Jersey Life* magazine and the off-Broadway play Two Detectives, and on numerous corporate and entertainment websites. He's traveled to 19 different countries but considers the great state of New Jersey the place to be.

Chris Leek

Chris Leek is the author of *Gospel of the Bullet*, *Nevada Thunder* and the short story collection *Smoke 'Em If You Got 'Em*. He is part of the team behind genre fiction imprint Zelmer Pulp and an editor at western fiction magazine, The Big Adios. He can be contacted via: www.zelmerpulp.com or at his blog: www.nevadaroadkill.blogspot.co.uk

Benoît Lièvre

Benoît Lelièvre is based in Montreal, Canada. He loves hardboiled stories, yet dabbles with several genres. When he is not writing fiction, he plays basketball, obsesses over sports stats and blogs at www.deadendfollies.com

Isaac Kirkman

Born in Greenville, South Carolina, Isaac Kirkman spent part of his youth in Sicily and part in the American hospital system, where he was diagnosed with Ehlers-Danlos Syndrome. He spent the following years lost in the streets before finding salvation at the Tucson Branch of The Writers Studio, which was founded by 2008 Pulitzer Winner, Philip Schultz in 1987.

The training and discipline Kirkman received at The Writers Studio helped him develop what he has dubbed Holy Noir—super-lyrical, socially conscious, Chillwave/Dreampop-style crime fiction.

His prose and poetry have appeared in Thuglit, Out of the Gutter, Shotgun Honey, Menacing Hedge, Apeiron Review, Counterexample Poetics, and The Dead Mule School of Southern Literature. He is a regular contributor to Zelmer Pulp Anthology series. Kirkman currently lives in Arizona where he spends his days devoted to dancing, spirituality and border-related human rights issues. He's an affiliate of Zelmer Pulp, The Southern Collective Experience, and The Last Ancients.

Brian Panowich

Brian is the Spinetingler award-nominated author of *Bull Mountain*, a southern crime saga coming out in summer, 2015 from Putnam Books. He's also Batman. Shhhh…

Chuck Regan

Chuck Regan is a part-time writer, full-time designer/illustrator working in the Philadelphia area. His short fiction has appeared in Shotgun Honey, The Big Adios, Space and Time Magazine, Gutter Books, Dark Corners Magazine, and in upcoming projects through Walrus Books. See more at www.cdregan.com.

Gareth Spark

Gareth Spark's prize-winning short fiction has appeared in Shotgun Honey, The Big Adios, Out of the Gutter, Near to the Knuckle, Line Zero and Deepwater Literary Review, among others.

Gareth has contributed stories to collections such as *The Shamus Sampler 2, Near to the Knuckle presents: Gloves off, Twelve Mad Men* (edited by Ryan Bracha), *Exiles: an outsider Anthology* (edited by Paul D. Brazill) and has a story in the soon to be released *Trouble in the Heartland*.

He lives in Whitby, Yorkshire and works a day job as a forklift driver. He is 35 years old.

Ryan Sayles

Ryan Sayles is the author of *Subtle Art of Brutality, Warpath, Goldfinches* and *That Escalated Quickly!* He has over two dozen stories published on websites, anthologies and in traditional print. *Subtle Art of Brutality* was nominated for top Indie novel at The House of Crime & Mystery's 2013 Readers' Choice Awards. Ryan is a founding member of Zelmer Pulp and the submissions editor at The Big Adios. He may be contacted at VitriolAndBarbies.wordpress.com

Made in the USA
Las Vegas, NV
14 June 2021